Red, White & Rodeo

BY

CASSANDRA JOELLE

For those who serve, those who wait, and the love that endures
the distance.

*"Greater love has no one than this: to lay down one's life for
one's friends." John 15:13 NIV*

CHAPTER 1
O SAY CAN YOU SEE

Savannah

"Honey, if you don't go out with him, I will." Dixie, my 73-year-old boss and owner of the Rodeo Diner, scooted me out of the kitchen where I had been hiding. Trying to avoid table 3 had proven to be impossible with Dixie's eyes that never missed a thing.

"He's adorable," she hollered out behind me, her voice carrying throughout the restaurant. My shaky hands brought the *Mountain Man Breakfast* to the guy sitting at the table, and I kept my eyes down.

"Can I get you anything else?" I asked, pulling extra napkins out of my apron and setting them on the table unsolicited. My eyes finally looked up, and I met the handsome gaze of his pale blue eyes.

"How about—" He was cut off as a marching band started up outside. Thankful for the interruption, I looked out and saw them dressed head to toe in red, white, and blue sequined outfits as they started performing the *Star-Spangled Banner.* The windows shook as their brass instruments rattled through the air, and the sun reflected off of their shining outfits, creating an instant need for sunglasses.

"Enjoy," I said, not even making an attempt for him to hear me over the music as I beelined back to the kitchen, where Dixie was making a fresh pot of coffee. Even with her back turned to me, I felt her eyes roll as her diamond jewelry glistened in the sterile light.

"Saved by the *marching band...*" I joked, considering that's not something you say every day, while knowing it wouldn't hit Dixie's funny bone. I sure got a kick out of it, however.

"You know, for a barrel racer, you sure have no guts, Savannah."

"I *do* have guts. I just don't know if I like him, that's all." Dixie nodded, and at first, I assumed she was understanding. Oh, how wrong I was always about that.

"What's not to like? Liam is *gorgeous.* Could be on the cover of *Farmers Weekly.* He's got a great job. Stand up family. Not to mention the boy is head over heels for *you.*" I looked out at him from the kitchen window. There was no denying he was handsome. Incredibly so, in fact. And Dixie was right about his family; they were wonderful people. I wasn't entirely convinced about the last part yet. After all, we'd barely spoken to each other at all. Other than the fact he'd been in here for the past few weeks, sitting in my section. I tried changing sections to see if he would notice, but Dixie always got involved, suddenly needing to take a break or go run an errand, and I was stuck with his table anyway. At this point, I'd accepted my fate and taken his table every time.

"I just don't feel a spark," I said to Dixie, relenting that I had virtually no reason not to like him, except that I just didn't. She shook her head.

"That's made up, you know." She elbowed me as Liam looked like he was running low on coffee. She handed me a fresh pot, straight from the machine. "Just one date. It wouldn't kill you to put yourself out there. He's not going anywhere, either." Dixie's words brought a flashback into my mind of watching my first love, Colter, board a bus for basic training. That was five years ago, and I hadn't seen him since. A mix of emotions ran through me as I held the handle of the coffee pot. Dixie's eyes sparkled as she looked at me with sadness in her eyes. "I'm sorry, honey. That was a low blow. I just want to see you happy, that's all." She walked away, her diamond-crusted bangles clinking as she swayed out of the kitchen and headed to the register.

I knew Dixie was coming from the right place. She was like the grandmother I had never had: a little pushy, set in her ways, and loved me fiercely. I had been working for her since I was sixteen—the same year I met Colter at the rodeo. In fact, it was here that we spent most of our last night together.

As I walked back to table 3, I looked at Liam, but I remembered when Colter sat at that very table the night before he left. He wanted us to spend more time together, so he insisted on coming in for my shift, ordering something every half an hour so I had to keep going back. I smiled at the memory, a shift of emotions coming to me as I reached Liam, who was now the recipient of my smile.

"Savannah," Liam spoke, putting his napkin down as he read the rhinestone name tag that was attached to my bejeweled dinette blouse. Dixie, a former rodeo queen, and now famous rodeo royalty, loved her sparkles.

"How was it?" I asked rhetorically while I picked up his empty plate.

"I hated it," he said with a laugh. For five years, I'd worked in the walls of this diner, and for five years, I'd learned to laugh at customers' jokes whether they warranted a laugh or not. It was just polite. So, as I cackled at the joke like a reflex, I caught eyes with Dixie at the register where she immediately winked at me. My cheeks reddened as it must have looked like I was flirting with this guy. I looked at Liam again; maybe deep down, I was. Dixie was right—he was very fine to look at. Suddenly, Jimmy, the dishwasher, walked over and took the plate out of my hand.

"We're short on dishes," he mumbled, which I knew was a blatant lie. I looked back at Dixie who suddenly appeared to be very engrossed with reciting the *Pledge of Allegiance*. She stood, hand over her heart, talking to a flag that swayed outside of the diner, her red lipstick matching the colors of the stripes. *Oh, she was good.*

"Thanks for coming in," I said, pulling out his guest check from my apron pocket. Just because I had no reason to walk away didn't mean I would linger here.

"I was wondering if you wanted to go out some time?" Liam finally worked up the courage to say the words that Dixie had been waiting for. I swayed in the moment; I had no reason to say no. Colter wasn't here, and he hadn't been in five years. I hadn't dated since, which Dixie teased me about constantly— that I was "breaking the hearts" of all of *her* contestants at the nightly rodeo. The contestants she claimed as her children because of how much she loved each and every one, as she did all the people in our town of Iron Spur. Was I going to stay single for the rest of my life? I hadn't considered that until this very second. Without a thought, I felt my shoulders shrug and my head nod.

"Sure," I said, nonchalantly.

"Don't make me twist your arm," Liam teased as he stood. His height towered over me. Was he *too* tall? Perhaps *too* handsome? As I painfully felt the comparison between his nearly-perfect looks to Colter's slanted smile, muscular but average height build, and the weighted, dramatic pull I felt towards him all those years ago, I wondered if anyone would ever compare.

"No, no arm twisting necessary." Dixie appeared, focused like a laser on Liam and me, now that she was done with her patriotism of the hour. "Where are you kids heading off to?" she asked to my wide-eyed response.

"I was thinking of a picnic and a movie. Or we could go see that musical act that's travelin' through town." Liam looked at me, waiting for an answer. This was all happening really fast.

"Oh, doesn't that sound *fun,*" Dixie gushed. Before I could suggest to Dixie that maybe she *should* be the one going out with him, I felt myself nodding in agreement. Why were my reflexes betraying me right now? It must have been because at work, I had no backbone. At work, I waited on the customers. Laughed hysterically at their jokes. Accepted their unsolicited life advice. Turned down innocent advances from elderly men with class and kindness, over and over again, as they repeated the behavior each day they returned. It was all part of the job. This, however, was very real, and not part of the job. Still, I would have been lying if I didn't agree that it sounded fun. The band, *Starry Eyed Cowboys,* played patriotic country music that I loved. They had toured here once before, years ago, and I missed it. This would be my chance. Sure, I could go without Liam, but what would really be the harm of one date?

CHAPTER 2
BY THE DAWN'S EARLY LIGHT

Savannah

Five Years Ago

Fireworks rang overhead as the national anthem blew through the mountain valleys.

"If this is what we do for July 1st this year, I can't even imagine what the 4th of July will bring," Colter smirked.

"You mean, your birthday celebration?" For Colter, who was never much into the July celebration, it was hilarious that his birthday was the Fourth. It was no secret he didn't care much for fireworks. Afterall, his dad was a veteran and always had a hard time with the noises. Their family dog, Ranger, wrestled with the sounds, too. But this year, Iron Spur, Wyoming had implemented drone fireworks shows. We got all of the sparkle, all of the excitement with none of the loud booms. None of the smoke, either. In this exceptionally dry part of the state, it didn't hurt to lower the fire risk in the heat of the summer. But mainly, it was a plan of action implemented for our large number of veterans and for that, I was thankful.

"Wow!" My eyes widened as a burst of red, white, and blue sparkles created an image of a cowboy boot in the sky above. The only crackling was a nearby stand selling kettle corn and over-salted popcorn. Colter put his arm around me as we sat on the tailgate of his red Chevy pickup truck. He squeezed me tight. In four days, Colter would be leaving Iron Spur for basic training. He was following in his dad's footsteps and becoming a soldier.

"I'm scared, Savannah." The softness of his voice sounded like that of a child. I took his hand in mine. Children ran by, giggling as they ate cotton candy. A little girl had two red bows in her hair as she twirled a sparkler through the air. Couples sat on large blankets and watched the fireworks as if they didn't have a care in the world. As if they weren't about to go into the unknown like Colter was.

Colter didn't say much the rest of the night. I was filling the void with idle chat—my song and dance that I did when people didn't speak. While I'd long been a self-diagnosed people-pleaser, tonight, that pleasing reached new heights. I wished to take all the fear away from the boy that I was in love with.

Colter and I met at the rodeo after his family moved here from Big Horn, Wyoming. Our town, like much of Wyoming, was pro-military, and we went above and beyond for the festivities for Veteran's Day, the 4th of July, and the huge program for Memorial Day that would bring the toughest to tears. The other draw for Colter's family was our rodeo, of course. While we didn't hold the designation of the rodeo capital of the world, like Big Horn, Wyoming, we competed fairly well in that aspect. I'd been barrel racing since I could ride a horse, and Colter had been bull riding since he was thirteen. That story wasn't unique to Iron Spur residents. Several people in our town had gone on to the Pro Rodeo Circuit and had roped, barrel raced, and ridden bulls all over the country. If it wasn't for my desire to stay in Iron Spur, I would have aimed to be one of those people.

As the drone fireworks show came to an end, the grand finale was an image of a cattle roping. Everyone clapped for the ones who put on the show.

The smell of chili dogs wafted over to where we sat in the truck. It was almost eleven at night, but this week was when the entire town shut down. Airport rules took effect, meaning if you wanted a hot dog or ice cream at 7 a.m. or midnight, you had it. While I'd never been much for a chili dog, the smell was appetizing, and Colter agreed.

A small carnival was set up in the Iron Spur town square. With fireworks banned in city limits, the sale of them was not, and several stands littered the streets. Colter asked if I wanted some sparklers after we got our hot dogs.

"I guess it's the only thing we can do in town," I said, with a smile and a shrug. The night was almost over, but I felt both of us wanting to savor the normalcy of this night. Savor the memories of being together. The day after his birthday, he was going to be gone, and I didn't know how long it would be until we were together again.

"I wish it was your birthday on the 4th," Colter grinned, handing me a lit sparkler that I twirled as we sat on a park bench. "You are the patriotic princess, after all." He took another bite of his chili dog. I shrugged.

"Colter, you can't say you are not patriotic. You're joining the military, after all." He nodded.

"Yeah, I do love my country. I'm just, I don't know..." He trailed off, staring into the distance. The streets were still buzzing with activity, while not a single business was open. "I'm nervous. Anything could happen. And I'm really sad about leaving you." He brushed my cheek with the back of his hand. My face lit up like a Christmas tree.

"God will protect you, Colter. I can feel it. And I'll spend all of my free time reminding you of that in my letters." I put my head on his chest after losing interest in my chili dog, setting it down in my lap. The tray was dangerously close to spilling on my white Miss Me jeans, my most bejeweled and special pair that I owned in a closet full of them. Colter went silent again. I looked up at him, expecting to see any trace of expression or thought, but I was returned with nothing. "What is it, Colter?" I pleaded.

"I don't want you to waste all of your free time on me," he said, with a sadness to his voice.

"Wasting?" I stood up from the bench, my hands on my hips. "Time spent on the one you love is never wasted." I pointed my finger at him and everything. His eyebrows shot up. By the time I realized what I'd said, it was too late. My face went hot. My mouth went dry. I was reaching for a soda, when I saw the one I had was empty. Someone walked by and just happened to be carrying a Big Gulp, and I was just about to ask for a sip when Colter started laughing.

"I knew you loved me," he said, standing up and taking me in his arms. I came up to his shoulders, which were naturally broad, something that all of the men in his family had. Colter was skinny but made of muscle. He squeezed me as tight as he could before releasing me again.

"I—didn't mean to say that." I looked down, my face still feeling beet red. But it wasn't a lie. It was the truest thing I've ever said. I knew people said that young love was fleeting and fe;t more intense than it really was, but second to Jesus, I'd never loved anything this much. I didn't see how things could change. I'd never been varied on things that I liked. How could I be on someone whom I loved?

"Does that mean it ain't true, darlin'?" Colter stood in front of me; in the lights of the town square, his brown eyes were as deeply colored as the brown of his felt cowboy hat. He held out his hands to me, and I put mine in his. We stared into each other's eyes; there was nowhere else I wouldn have rather been.

"No. It's the truth," I whispered.

"What was that? I didn't hear you," he smiled. He wasn't going to let me off this easily, I could tell.

"It's the truth," I said, this time a little louder. We were gaining the attention of the kettle corn vendor just a few yards away. People were starting to pack up and go home. Kids with blue tongues from the blue raspberry slushie machines were walking by with their tongues sticking out at everyone. Colter kept his gaze on me. I wanted to remember what this felt like forever.

"I love you, Savannah." His words pierced my heart like an arrow. Electricity ran between our bodies as we held hands. A garbage collector walked by and picked up my half-eaten chili dog from the bench. But while all of this was happening around us, our love held all of the promise and devotion in the world. "And I'm going to love you forever." I felt faint from joy. Colter Hays loved me! Colter and I were going to be together forever! Once he got out of the military, surely he would be right back here with me, and we would pick up as normal. I couldn't wait for our future together. I couldn't wait for him to be back. For now, we still had a few days left to spend together, and I was certain we would make each one sweeter than the last.

CHAPTER 3
WHAT SO PROUDLY WE HAIL'D

Savannah

Five Years Ago

I was so wrong about everything. Between Colter's parents, his grandparents coming down from Big Horn, and my shifts at the Rodeo Diner, Colter and I barely had any time together on his few remaining days. Then, I got a fateful call that Dixie needed me at the Diner on the afternoon of the 4th.

"Savannah, we will be the only business open in town. You know how much people like to sit indoors to watch the parade from the comfort of a cushioned booth and air conditioning. You are fixin' to make a fortune in tips today, sweetheart." Dixie pleaded with me to come in, though we both knew I was going to say yes. She was a little shorthanded this month with another girl leaving to spend July with her cousins in Oklahoma.

"Okay, I'll do it. But can you reserve a booth for Colter? Today is our last day together and..." I stopped before breaking down in tears.

"Of course, sweetheart. Here. You hear that?" A tray was heard touching a table. "I got that fancy reserved sign, like the five-star establishment that we are, on the end table. Any break you get, you sit with your honey." I wiped the tears that escaped my eyes and thanked her, getting off the phone to get ready for my impending shift.

"Where are you off to?" my mom asked, as I waltzed through the kitchen in my diner uniform. "I usually don't expect to see that many rhinestones before noon," she teased about my apron. Dixie, being rodeo queen royalty, liked things sparkling, and my uniform was no different.

"I got called into work," I said, the tears coming back as my mom took me in for a deep hug.

"It's going to be alright, Savannah." She petted the top of my head, running her fingers through my strawberry blonde hair. "Time will go by so fast. He will be back before you know it." I nodded.

"Thanks, Mom. Well, I better get to the diner. You know that Billy is burning ditches today, and I'm sure I'll be stuck in traffic from all the fire trucks coming to put it out." Billy was our elderly neighbor who always burned his fields and ditches in the heat of the summer and the windiest days of the year. It was a long-running joke that they called him "Burning Billy." Despite him never calling for a burn permit, the county hadn't charged him a single time for coming to his aid. He was just so loveable, no one had the heart to do it. That being said, with it being a very low humidity day and with a casual wind of fifteen miles per hour picking up, it was almost guaranteed I was going to be passing trucks on the way to work.

*****

That day at the diner was a whirlwind. Colter didn't show up until an hour before my shift ended, which by how busy I was, I was thankful. I wouldn't have been able to pay much attention to him, let alone wait on his table.

Dixie had just pulled out three piping hot cherry pies from the oven when I walked in the side door. My hair was pulled back in a low pony with a slight curl in the bottom. I was wearing an oversized bright red bow on the hair tie that was so wide, you could see it from looking at me head on. I knew Dixie would love it, as it was crusted in gems.

The smell of the pies made my mouth water. One pie was already on the counter, perfectly sliced with a large bowl of fresh whipped cream sitting beside it.

"Save me a slice? This is Colter's favorite," I said, adjusting my sparkly apron around my waist. Dixie agreed, immediately plating the largest piece and giving me a wink. She put it in the oversized fridge so it wouldn't be left out.

As soon as I stepped onto the floor, a crowd of people came in. I had spent the next several hours hearing bits and pieces of the parade through the chatter of the patrons, from the marching bands to the forest service horses demonstrating their skills, to a man dressed up in an Uncle Sam costume walking around on stilts. The parades here were a sight to be seen, and despite my disappointment that I had to work today, this was my first job and my first summer working, and I reminded myself I was the low man on the totem pole. I was going to be the first to be called in when Dixie needed someone. And I was also incapable of saying no to people who needed me, so there were problems to be had everywhere.

I just kept wishing it hadn't been today. If it wasn't the 4th of July, Colter wouldn't be leaving tomorrow. I wouldn't be in a huge rush to get through all of these customers so I could leave my shift. I wouldn't be mentally and emotionally preparing to have my heart broken at the end of the day.

Finally, he walked in. It was one of those moments when the whole diner felt like it went quiet. Like everyone in the world had been anticipating him as much as I had. My heart started doing that thing where it feels like a butterfly using a jump rope, somewhere in between indigestion and requiring medical attention.

"Colter," I said, practically flinging my body towards him. He smiled, but it didn't reach his eyes as he took me in his arms. I didn't let myself get lost in his hug. Not here. Not when I was on display for everyone in my town to watch me. The hug was brief, over before it started, which hurt almost as much as if I hadn't hugged him at all.

"I'm sorry I couldn't come earlier. My parents wanted to do the whole parade thing," he shrugged. "And my grandparents wanted me to eat cake and ice cream for breakfast, like when I was a kid!" Finally, he let out a real, rambunctious laugh.

"Always the grandparents," I laughed with him. "That's really a shame you've had your fill of sugar today, because I have a huge piece of Dixie's cherry pie in the cooler. I guess I'll have to eat it myself." Colter's eyes opened large.

"No, no. I better take that off your hands," he smirked. I nodded and showed him to his table towards the back of the diner. Dixie had saved him the most private one, which I was thankful. After he sat down, a family waved to me, motioning that they needed more coffee. I smiled and nodded.

"I'll be right back with your pie," I winked, picking up the heavy pitcher of freshly made coffee and pouring it for the family at table five. Next thing I knew, three other people requested refills, and two asked for the check. Jimmy, the dishwasher/busser was delivering food to tables to help out in the rush. As I passed the tables, one woman needed a side of ranch dressing as soon as her plate was set in front of her. I nodded, and my eyes went to Colter, who from here had his back to me. He was alone, staring at the seat in front of him. Tomorrow, he was leaving and here I was, in the last place I wanted to be, but my hands were tied. I didn't want to lose this job. Dixie needed me. I didn't see any other options.

Finally, after several minutes of running around condiments, drinks, coffee, and checks, I served Colter his pie, with a heaping serving of whipped cream.

"I'm sorry to keep you waiting," I said with a frown, sliding into the booth in front of him. As much as I wanted to sit beside him, I wanted to look at him. To memorize his face a little more. To take him all in as much as I could.

"I'd wait forever, Savannah." His eyes looked sad. My heart felt like it was pinched. The reality was setting in. Dixie walked over to the table as Colter picked up his fork.

"Not so fast, boy," she teased, pulling out a candle, poking it into the pie, and taking a matchbook out of her apron. "I heard it was your birthday." She lit it, a bright dancing flame burning quickly over the pie, and said, "make a wish," before she winked at me and walked back into the kitchen.

"I wish I didn't have to go tomorrow," he said, the flame lighting up his face with a warm glow.

"You can't tell me, or it won't come true," I said, softly, knowing that short of a meteor hitting the Earth, Colter would be leaving tomorrow on that Greyhound bus. After a moment, the wax started dripping into his pie. He blew it out, hesitantly, and without looking at me again, took his first bite. His expression told me it helped immensely.

"This is the best pie I've ever had," he said through his chewing.

"That's right it is," Dixie hollered from the kitchen window. The ample whipped topping was starting to lose its stability, turning into a lovely cream, pooling around the pie. He put a bite onto the spoon and held it out to me. Just one taste and Colter was right: Dixie outdid herself on this recipe. Not only were the cherries perfectly ripe—likely, hand chosen for perfection—but the body of the pie had the slightest hints of cinnamon and pineapple. I wouldn't have paired the flavors together myself, but tasting this now, I was tempted to buy the rest of the pie and eat the whole thing for dinner.

Before we knew it, the pie was gone, and my shift was ending. I had to leave the booth to help a few more patrons as they shuffled in and out, but when the several hours of parading finally ended, the crowds started to move on elsewhere, too.

"Why don't you go on and have some fun?" Dixie said, motioning to the door. I looked outside and saw the sky was already dimming in the early evening.

"Thank you, Dixie." I took off my apron in two seconds flat, swinging it over my shoulder.

"No, thank you for coming in, Savannah. You've been a real lifesaver." She handed me a $100 dollar bill. I was blown away by the gesture, thanking her as I eagerly accepted, and I tore back over to Colter.

"I'm all done here. Want to go pick a spot to watch the fireworks?" I asked, looking forward to having his arms around me as we sat next to each other on the tailgate of his truck. But he shrugged.

"I don't know if I'm in the mood," he said, the sadness again present in his voice. He gave me one glance and knew I was upset to hear that. "I have another idea."

CHAPTER 4
AT THE TWILIGHT'S LAST GLEAMING

Savannah

Five Years Ago

While the entire town of Iron Spur was sitting in the fields south of the city square watching the fireworks, Colter drove me to the rodeo grounds.

"The rodeo was earlier in the day today. Remember?" Usually, it was at eight in the evening, except today. They hosted it in the heat of the day, as the cowboys that competed in the pro-rodeo circuit had to travel in between each ride. Depending on their sponsors, some of them had chartered planes, flying them from state to state and everywhere in between. This week was the big money week for a lot of them.

"I know. Just... Do you trust me, Savannah?" He held out his hand to me in the bucket seat. I took it.

"Of course I trust you, Colter."

"Okay then." He pulled into a spot by the horse trailers and one of the people in charge of the animals walked over.

"Colter." They shook hands through the window of his truck, Colter got out, shutting the door behind him, and the two men talked for a few minutes. I only heard bits and pieces through the door.

"*You got it, man*," was all I picked up, as Colter walked around to my side and opened the door for me. The man walked off and reappeared a few minutes later with two beautiful horses, one white, one cream colored. Both of them looked like they'd just gone through the 4th of July parade, as they were covered in red, white, and blue regalia. They each had red sparkle cuffs around all four legs, glittery bridles, and gorgeous, rich leather saddles that looked like they would be a dream to ride on. I looked at the horses in awe, before looking to Colter with confusion. He answered before I could ask.

"How about a stroll through the empty streets of downtown, while the town is at the fireworks show?" My heart leapt at the gesture. I may have only been sixteen, but this was the most romantic thing that I could ever imagine happening to me. I practically jumped into the saddle of the nearest horse, putting my cowgirl boot into the stirrup so fast, no one had to tell me twice. The rodeo area had its main lights off, but streetlamps illuminated the parking area. Under the glow, the horses shined like their fur was made of a sateen.

"Whose horses are these?" I asked the man who handed me the reins, once I was in the saddle.

"These belong to me. I rented them to the rodeo queen today for the parade. They are all a part of the queen's court." He gave me a toothy grin. "I'm Richard Sorrel, the stock contractor." He held out his hand, and I shook it.

"Savannah Lane," and his eyes lit up.

"Savannah?" He pulled back his head. "I know you! You won in your age group last month in Barrel Racing." I nodded nonchalantly. God always kept me humble, and for every win I had, I had dozens of losses. "You're going to do great things, kiddo."

"We will have them back in an hour," Colter said, getting into the saddle of the other horse with ease. Richard nodded and waved us off.

"I'll be here watering the herd till late. Have fun."

Cruising the downtown streets of Iron Spur at night was already fun. Old-fashioned marquee lights lit up several blocks with a romantic glow that only hundreds of tiny bulbs could give. The warmth of the summer nights made it comfortable to be out in a short sleeve shirt if you wanted. I didn't do shorts very often, as I was always on a horse or about to be, but July was warm enough that we could if we wanted to. The best part about downtown in the summer was the smell of cotton candy that was always wafting through the air.

Now, coming down to the empty, lit-up streets on a glittering horse felt like a fever dream. A core memory. Something I would never let far from my mind. Every piece of the horse's tinsel, sparkle, and regalia was caught by the lights. And every step we took felt more magical; like the world was entirely ours.

"I love you, Savannah," Colter said, as he reached out his right hand to take my left. And there we were, riding horses side by side, holding hands on our last night together before everything changed.

*****

He wrote a handful of letters for a few months following his departure, but he never again spoke the heartfelt words, telling me he loved me. They were mostly filled with encouragement for my barrel racing and words about staying focused for my future. If a stranger read them, they would have never known that this boy held my hand under the starry sky of my parents' ranch while we sat on the porch, where he told me how afraid he was. How he was doing this all to better the future he could have. A better future for us. How he wanted me to wait for him. But starting with the first letter that I received, and up until he finished boot camp, his tone was completely changed.

At first, I expected to see him after the ten weeks of boot camp. At least briefly. Wasn't that the usual? As heartbreaking as it was, the week of his graduation ceremony, I was back in school, and we had a big rodeo clinic that same weekend. It was crushing to me. But I held on hope that he would still return after all of his training was completed.

After boot camp, he moved on to advanced training. Training for infantry went on for what felt like forever. I prayed for him every day and night that he would learn the skills he needed to stay alive. That he would not lose himself. To come back to me. Then, finally, he was in his last week of training. Christmas was just around the corner. My hope was high that I would see him.

While my dad was placing our Christmas tree in its stand, the smell of the freshly cut pine tree wafting through their ranch house, I heard the mail truck. My mind was focused on Colter as usual, and the thought implanted in my mind that maybe today, there would be a letter. Things were getting less frequent. I was still writing to him as much as I promised, but few responses were coming back, the weight of which was crushing me more by the day.

"I'll be right back," I announced to my parents, who nodded. They knew exactly where I was going off to, and no comment needed to be made on the matter. I could sense they had been trying to keep me distracted the last several months. That they knew how I had been waiting for letters like my life depended on it. One night, I overheard them discussing that they wished I hadn't ever gotten involved with Colter so I could have avoided this situation. While I understood the sentiment, Colter and I were made for each other. From the moment I met him, I never wanted to do this life without him by my side.

The cold and snowy walk to the mailbox brought me reflection and prayer. *Lord, let me hear from him. Let me know that he's okay.* As I pulled the metal lever on the oblong box, my heart stopped. A single white envelope lay inside, upside down. With shaky hands, I grabbed it, holding it close. If this wasn't from him, I would be devastated. Flipping it over, I saw my name on the letter. I saw the scribble of his name at the top. It was missing a return address. The stamp from the location had been damaged from the snow. I couldn't read what remained clear. The stamps were from a foreign desert in an alphabet I didn't recognize. It was so lightweight that I wondered how it even made it here at all. How it didn't just blow away in the wind.

I pulled out the half page. The ink was smeared; a left-handed sign he had been writing fast. While the words didn't resonate immediately, and while the letter at first seemed feather light, it now held the weight of the world it came from, thousands of miles away. *"Don't wait for me."* Colter had been immediately deployed.

I reread it hundreds of times, just to be sure. I cried my eyes out for days, while Christmas came and went, and wallowed in the darkness of depression, but slowly, I started to come out of it after spending time in the Bible and reading the book of Ruth. She was a young widow, and that's how I felt. But at the end of the day, Colter was still alive and so was I. So, I prayed. I prayed hard that I could move on from this pain.

CHAPTER 5

WHOSE BROAD STRIPES AND BRIGHT STARS

Savannah

Five Years Ago

A week later was my first barrel race. It was pink night for breast cancer awareness, and Daisy was going to be wearing her pink glitz bridle, and I would don my matching fringe chaps that had the same sparkle on them. The usual nerves ran through me, as I had before any race, but there were new stakes today. Colter was gone. He had just broken up with me. That night, I was barrel racing with the new reality of him no longer in my life.

I will always remember that day. My mother came out on the front porch with a pitcher of iced tea and watched me finish Daisy's mane. "Tonight will be a special race. I have a really good feeling about it." She beamed.

"You always say that." I smiled at her.

"And I'm always right. You have the trophies to prove it!" It was true, my father had to build a new shelf in my room just to accommodate, but my mother still brought them out and would incorporate them into her decor, so they were scattered around the house.

"I'm about ready, I just need to change. Can you let Dad know?" She stood and nodded, walking to the other side of the porch and ringing the large bell usually reserved for emergencies if he was out somewhere on the range. We waited to hear the loud claps of his horse's steps, but nothing. A few minutes later he walked onto the porch from inside of the house.

"You were inside this whole time?" I looked at him in amazement; he was wearing his cowboy finest: nice jeans, a button up pink shirt with a black bolero, and his white cowboy hat. "I wouldn't miss pink night for the world." He tipped his hat.

There were four racers ahead of me and only two of them got times that would even consider competition; my average time was around eighteen seconds, and tonight, I'd need to do it in sixteen if I wanted to win. "We've got our work cut out for us, Daisy. Do you think we can do it?" My horse nudged me gently with her nose, telling me that she was ready.

The voice on the loudspeaker had its usual cowboy drawl, but the words surprised me. I'd been so busy competing this year that I let my mother keep track of my points. And to think I was worried about not being good enough; I could have a chance at NFR? Looking up at the grandstands, my mother smiled at me expectantly. This must have been what they were going on about earlier. What a special night it would be for me, to hear this news. It only added to my nerves, as I got into the saddle and stepped out into the area while the crowd went wild.

I always started each race with the same move, with the right barrel first. We tore around the right barrel, my pulse rattling my ears louder than the crowd cheering. My hat was pulled down low, and with it blocking out many of the people in attendance, I pretended they were not here. It was just me and my horse, no different than at home in the pasture with our makeshift course set up. Daisy raged on to the next barrel, high center. A slight crosswind blew over me, and I felt the speed in the air. This would be my record breaking, career-making time. We had one barrel left to go; the bottom left. We'd done this course a million times. Heck, I'd won enough here in my little town to sack away for my future. This barrel was no match for us. But something happened. I felt my saddle shift ever-so-slightly, a movement someone else may not have noticed, and in the motion of this, I mistakenly pulled right when I should've pulled left. It was against my own instincts. It was against Daisy's instincts. Overcorrecting can get you killed; it can get your horse killed. Daisy lost her footing and the rest happened in slow motion. We began to tip to the side, the wrong side which was into the barrel. I knew it was my mistake; this wasn't my horse's fault, but it was time to bail. I quickly did what I was trained to do and pulled my feet out of the stirrups. My legs were now just floating on top of the saddle as I leap-frogged on top of it, miraculously landing next to Daisy, both of us unscathed.

I had no tangible injuries. Daisy was fine. I didn't get a score that night, but I also didn't get injured. I was thankful to God that my only wounds were emotional, including the broken heart I carried.

Through everything that had happened, I was so thankful for my parents. Now, as I also mourned the loss of my latest score at the rodeo, they were very supportive during my breakup with Colter. My father thought maybe he'd met a woman over there, which at first didn't help my feelings at all. My mother chimed in that maybe he was just afraid, and that we should pray for him. So, that's what we did; every night as a family, we added him into our prayers.

Slowly, the shift went back as the months passed, and we resumed our day-to-day lives. Daisy and I started training harder in my arena. My mother had scoffed when I turned down three proposals for prom, but I wasn't interested in dating anyone else. I wasn't ready to even pose next to a guy who wasn't Colter. I just wanted to be home, relishing in the peace and quiet of our mountains in Wyoming, smelling the beautiful sagebrush after the summer downpours, and watching Daisy frolic around with the herd of quarter horses, while I listened to thunder clapping in the distance.

It wasn't lost on me how special it was to live like this. And with this being all I'd ever known, on our monthly trips to Denver, Colorado for clothes shopping and other larger ranch necessities you couldn't find around here, I felt like I was suffocating in the vast lands of asphalt and people, that sprawled as far as the eye could see. Iron Spur, Wyoming was my home and the only place I ever wanted to be. And deep down, I'd be lying if I said I didn't hold out hope that Colter would return one day. I wondered what I would be like then. I wondered what he would be like. How old he would be. Would he still feel the same? The only thing I knew was that my feelings for him would never change. All I had left was the memories of our last night together on the 4th of July, trotting down the deserted downtown on sparkling horses, their regalia glittering in the light of the marquees.

CHAPTER 6
THROUGH THE PERILOUS FIGHT

Savannah

Present Day

The windchimes rang through the middle of the day as I raced my horse, Daisy, around the pasture, savoring the wind in my hair on my day off from the diner. My mother watched from the kitchen window, surely keeping a list of critiques for me on my form, while she washed freshly picked vegetables from her garden. I would smile as I passed by with each stride, as she often said not enough barrel racers smile.

"No, they don't smile enough, as they are too busy staying on the horse." I would tease her, giving her my best smile.

"I can't help that my daughter has a winning smile." She threw her arms up, sincerely believing that shiny, white teeth would improve a score based on speed. The smell of the freshly baked bread with homemade butter wafted through my senses, reminding my stomach it was time to eat, and I best go find my father if I wanted to be sitting down for lunch before dinner time.

My father would always be found either whittling away at something in his loafing shed, working with his cattle, or simply watching the irrigation for its inevitable problems. I'd always tease him that a watched pot never boils, but he'd come back with something more serious. "And I get one rock in the hose from the irrigation canal, and this whole system seizes up; the hay will die and the cows soon to follow."

"That's dark, Pop. Mom made lunch, and it's ready if you can afford to step away with stakes as high as they are." He'd usually hesitate but was always inside within a few minutes to eat his meal before returning to the pasture again.

"From the moment they turn the canal on, I become a widow for the next five months. I live with his shadow. But he's spent his life working this land, and while you'd think it would get easier over the years, for your father, I'm afraid it's only gotten harder," my mother shared with me once, as I dried the dishes she washed, looking out the window. Much of her life was spent in front of that window it seemed, and sometimes I wondered if she was content.

With the cattle, there was as much work to do for the ranch wife as there was for the husband. While they would share many duties, such as calving, counting, and the cattle drives, much of the work, my father just didn't have the mind for. Such as record keeping; covering all things necessary for breeding and selling. She also handled the advertising for their bloodline of cattle, which was popular among those in the market for buying, as their angus was known for their large stature and impressive weights. One head would often sell for thousands, and that animal would often become the bull that started a rancher's career. But it wasn't always roses and piles of money; in fact, quite the opposite. As my father liked to say, "...if you want to have a million dollars from angus, start with a billion." Though he was humble, he worked harder than most and managed to tuck a modest sum away for their retirement, which with every year that passed by, I reminded him was approaching.

The sandwiches my mom prepared today were piled high with meats and cheeses, along with fresh peppers and sprouts from her garden. The aioli glaze was thick and creamy. My mother was an excellent cook. When we finished with lunch,

I went back outside. Though I'd long since moved out on my own, my favorite way to spend a day off was at my family ranch.

An impressive acreage set in the foothills of a beautiful mountain range, without neighbors, without concrete for miles and miles. A meager dirt road that my father meticulously maintained eventually would get you to town if you followed it long enough; and then you'd find anything you'd need to reasonably sustain life, such as a church, grocery store, hospital, and the rodeo arena. What more did someone really need?

*****

The date with Liam was fine. He was a complete gentleman, picking me up from my apartment with a small bouquet of meticulously arranged flowers.

"These reminded me of you," he spoke softly, as he handed them to me. A mix of pastel colors captivated my senses as I smelled their strong sweet fragrance.

"Thank you," I said, walking back inside to put them in water. Liam waited at the door. "You're welcome to come in," I said, waiving him over the threshold. He walked in slowly, running his hand through his curly blonde locks.

"Nice place," he said, looking around, not mentioning that his head was almost touching the ceiling of my cramped apartment. He walked over to my mantel which displayed a few family photos and some of my rodeo belt buckles that I'd won in the last few years. There was enough gold on that mantel to buy a house, but the pride of the prizes was everything.

"There," I said, placing the vase of flowers on my tiny, built-in table that had cushions like a small diner booth, except these ones weren't covered with a glittery vinyl like the ones at work.

"You ever think you'll do the whole 'rodeo queen' thing?" he asked, as if it was just that easy. But Dixie had been badgering me about that for years, wanting me to follow in her footsteps. I nodded.

"As a matter of fact, I've just thrown my hat in the ring," I said with an eye roll.

"You sound like you regret it already," Liam added, the tone similar to when he asked me out, and I replied with a shrug. I stood a little straighter and rethought my actions.

"I've been in a little bit of a funk," I admitted, thinking I might as well get it out now. "I feel like I need something new to mix it up. Dixie has been hoping I would try the rodeo queen thing for years, so, here I am."

"That's a heavy statement," Liam said, going quiet. I didn't worry about the implications of it. I just led with my heart.

"You are not part of that funk," I lied. At least, partially. I wasn't quite sure yet how I felt.

"Okay," Liam's eyes lit up. "We better get if we are going to make it to the show," he pointed towards the door. I picked up my purse and followed, where I spent the rest of the evening in the comfort of his sweet company.

One date turned into two, which turned into two weeks of dates. I found myself having fun. I found myself enjoying the attention from Liam. Dixie was on cloud nine every time he came by. She would beam with pride as she referred to him as "Savannah's boyfriend." On the third week of seeing him, Liam overheard Dixie say this, and he looked at me with a grin.

"Does that mean you are saying yes?" he asked, taking my hand as he slid into the usual booth.

"Saying yes to what?" I asked.

"To being my girl," he smiled sweetly. His girl. As in, belonging to Liam. My head started to spin as I considered the question. Before I toppled over, I slid into the opposite side of the both and held onto the sparkle seats with dear life. Dixie walked over and looked me up and down.

"Are you expecting that seat to fall out underneath you? Or eject you into the open sky?" I shook my head, feeling sweat bead up on my forehead.

"I—" I kept shaking.

"I think she's having a panic attack," Dixie said with concern, pulling me out of the booth and walking me to her office in the back. The room had teal paisley wallpaper and smelled like the doughy cinnamon rolls that she baked every morning. The walls were lined with her crowns from being the reigning rodeo queen back in the day. She sat me down on the plush, pink leather couch and pulled out a paper bag. "Breathe into this," she said, handing it to me. I did as she said, not feeling any better. She shrugged. "I've never had a panic attack myself, even when I found out the Iron Spur Rodeo Association was not going to let me keep running for queen, so 'someone else' could have a chance." She used air quotes dramatically with her long, hot pink nails, and a diamond or turquoise ring on every finger. "But this is something that they used to love to incorporate on 90's melodramas." Dixie rolled her eyes. "I sure do miss my soap operas. *Thank goodness for reality television.*"

When my breathing normalized, Dixie took the bag from my hand.

"I don't know what that was about," I said, tears running halfway down my cheeks.

"I think I have an idea," she said, leaning back on the couch.

"Oh yeah? Feel free to share," I teased, thankful for not having worn any makeup that day. My strawberry blonde eyelashes were drenched.

"You think that going out with Liam means you are betraying Colter." Her words rang like the Liberty Bell. I nodded, a few tears sneaking out of the corners of my eyes again. "Well, that's just not the case, Savannah. Colter left here, and though he took your heart with him, you exist. He broke things off, and I'm sorry. I so wish that could work out for you. But it's time to move on." I sat in the aftermath, praying on the words. *God, was it time to move on?*

The sound of firecrackers in front of the diner made us both jump up. "Those darn kids are at it again," Dixie groaned and swayed back out to the front. I watched her, considering my theory that even if this whole place went up in flames, she would still keep her soft pace. There was no hustle in her movements.

As I gathered myself, I checked my reflection in the mirror. If there had been any redness to my cheeks, it had passed. My eyes were a little red, but otherwise, I looked acceptable. I went back out to the front and felt relief that Liam was still there, which surprised me. Both feeling the relief meant I wanted him there, right? And the fact that he stayed made me feel remorseful that I had just cried at his question of being his girlfriend.

"I'm sorry, Liam, I—" Liam cut me off.

"I know about Colter, Savannah." He stood, making it easier for me to avoid eye contact, as my gaze came to the center of his chest. Hearing him speak Colter's name made it feel different. Made it feel more of a reality that Colter was gone from Iron Spur. Gone from my life. I had no idea where he was, but I knew he was still alive. News like that would travel too fast for me to miss that. But that's all I knew, and if that was the bar for information, then maybe I was as pathetic as I felt right now. I leaned in and gave Liam a hug, watching Dixie tell the kids shooting off Piccolo Pete fireworks in front to get lost. Never mind that the sheriff was sitting in a booth eating his lunch. Even he knew Dixie would be more effective than he could.

"I do want to be your girl," I said into Liam's chest, and he pulled up his arms and hugged me back, while I felt new emotions wash over me. Colter was gone. Liam knew about him.

Everything was out in the open, the darkness of my heart had been brought into the light, and now I had been presented with a second chance at love.

CHAPTER 7
O'ER THE RAMPARTS WE WATCH'D

Savannah

The sound of crickets was singing through the valley as Daisy and I left the ranch. This route was our usual ride—we'd head North until we made it to the mountain meadow overflowing with wildflowers, where she would graze, and I would contemplate my life and talk to God for the rest of the day. Only close to dinner time would we return to the pasture, and I'd take my truck and return back to my one-bedroom apartment that overlooked the rodeo grounds. This day was no different. But somewhere in my mind, things had changed. I wasn't a teenager anymore.

When we returned back to the pasture in the evening, my mother waved me inside.

"Savannah, will you come in for a minute? I want to show you something." She was beaming a beautiful smile, ear to ear. I nodded and went up the rickety wooden steps of their wrap-around porch. The glass doorknob of the old farmhouse felt warm from the sun in my hand as I went inside. In the entryway of the home, it opened up to a large living room, where my mother was holding up a pair of red, white, and blue leather chaps that were covered in rhinestones. Memories flooded my mind of the last time she surprised me with chaps, but I was getting really good at pushing those thoughts far from my mind.

"Look what I found in Denver yesterday!" Her excitement was contagious, as I tore the chaps out of her hand and hugged her.

"They are so perfect! Thank you, Mom." I was nearly jumping up and down from the thrill of how pretty they were. So much so that I toppled over when trying them on, hitting the side of my head on the coffee table.

"Savannah, are you okay? What is it about new chaps that make you go sideways?" My mother gave me a concerned look as I lay on the floor of the living room, contemplating why they still had the same green carpet from the 80's, when this house was hiding beautiful wood floors underneath. But the carpet made for a soft landing, so I couldn't be too upset.

"I'm okay," I said, noticing she wasn't reaching out to help me up. I laughed and got to my feet, starting again with the chaps. "These will be perfect with my outfit on the 4th!" I donned them, walking around and listening to the slapping sound of the leather, as I twirled around the living room. Just then, my dad walked in and let out a low whistle.

"Aren't you a vision in patriotism?" he said, crossing his arms.

"This is better than the junior high school dance," my mom added, to my dad's laughter.

"Savannah, do you remember when you picked out a dress at the secondhand store, and we didn't realize, until the night of, that it had a tear in the backside?" As if I could ever forget. Not remembering that would be a real red flag, but I didn't say this. I knew how this played out, and I let my parents enjoy the teasing while I smiled and rolled my eyes.

"You had to wear that sequin number instead," my mom giggled. "It actually looked better than the one you picked out, though." She put her hands up in the air. The sequin dress they were referring to was from a costume party my mom attended in the late 90's, where she was half of a Sonny and Cher duo. Thankfully, the dress fit me brilliantly and other than looking like a shiny gold disco ball all night, I had a great time.

"I better get going. I'm meeting Liam for dinner at Oscar's tonight," I said hesitantly. It was weird thinking of the fact that I had a boyfriend, and I was still getting used to the idea of dating again. But his persistent pursuit of me had been fun. And I was enjoying the buzz of this life change. My parents both smiled and nodded.

"Your mom and I just want you to be happy, Savannah. If Liam helps in this effort, we are pleased as punch. Bring him over sometime so we can meet him." As my dad spoke, I saw that both he and my mom were still walking on eggshells with me regarding my dating life. Neither one of them had ever said Colter's name in years.

As I drove my ranch truck back to my apartment, I noticed all of the 4th of July decorations that Iron Spur had started to put up today, and it wasn't just the stores. Homes were decorated with red, white, and blue bunting. Fresh flags were flapping high in the air, blowing in the constant gentle breeze. Some said that even our weather was patriotic, never letting the flags go down.

Fireworks stands again littered the streets. The glow of the day was still here. The biggest reason why I loved the warm summer nights was because you could stay out till half past eight and still have daylight. You could feel the kiss of the warmth on your skin while you absorbed as much outside time as possible. Then, after the sun went down, you could stroll the streets that were filled with people donning western wear, even if for the first time in their lives, as they headed towards the rodeo. And that's where the real fun began.

I started my career in barrel racing when I was little. My dad set up a small arena for me to practice in with a pony named Strawberry. We didn't go very fast, but I learned the ropes of the sport, and I'd never looked back.

Liam wasn't a cowboy, but more of a farmer. He had a huge garden, which I knew my mom would get a kick out of since she too was a gardener. I always saw myself with a cowboy. Well, let me rephrase: I always saw myself with Colter, who was a cowboy, a bull rider, and the best this town had ever seen, even in his young age. He had every opportunity to ride through the rodeo circuit, but instead, he joined the Army.

The thoughts of Colter were suddenly running rampant like a bull in my mind. But instead of putting up the guardrails of my heart, I wondered if perhaps now that I had another boyfriend, I could safely think of him. My cheeks flushed at just the thought of Colter, and my stomach felt twisted as I realized I couldn't safely think of him without feeling overcome with heartbreak, sadness, and *wanting.* The desire I had, and still very much had to be with this guy, was overwhelming.

Liam doesn't deserve this, I thought to myself. He is a gem of a guy. Persistent. Thoughtful. He loved Iron Spur, Wyoming as much as I did. He didn't plan on going anywhere. I didn't have to wait for him to leave. We were compatible on these fronts. I enjoyed his company. He was kind and respectful. Therefore, I thought he was perfectly reasonable to date. Liam was cute, too. He had curly blonde hair and big blue eyes. He was a little pale from working his IT job indoors all day, but with his farming on the weekends, that may change. I liked to tease him that he only came out at night, like some weird creature of the night, but it was true. If only he could tan in the moonlight.

When I got home, Liam was parked outside already. I gave him a slow smile and found myself wishing he wasn't already here, which filled me with regret instantly.

"Hi," I said, getting out of my truck. "I just need a few minutes to change." Liam smiled excitedly, and I noticed a huge bouquet of pink flowers on the passenger seat of his Chevy. He reached over and handed it to me out of his truck window.

"You better put these in water while you're in there," he smiled earnestly. I thanked him for the gesture, taking in a deep breath of the heavily-fragrant flowers. They smelled divine. My hands felt shaky as I walked up the stairs to my apartment door, feeling Liam's eyes on me. I knew part of that was because I was hungry. Yes, food would help. But something else was different. I just didn't know what.

CHAPTER 8
WERE SO GALLANTLY STREAMING

Savannah

"You look like the next winner," Dixie said, as I stood on the pedestal of her office in the dress she got me for the Iron Spur Rodeo Queen Pageant. It was bright red, which made my strawberry blonde hair pop. The long sleeves had small amounts of fringe, which was something I hadn't seen on a formal dress before. It had a boat neckline, and the subtle sequins would be shining as brightly as a disco ball on stage. A beautiful American flag belt with a large shiny silver buckle accented the waist.

"Which hat do you like best?" I asked her. Dixie was sponsoring my entry, which meant she bought the dress and had a say in everything I wore. I didn't mind; the biggest reason I was doing it at all was because she would guide me from start to finish. Besides, it was fun. To feel beautiful and wear glamorous outfits was fun. Having a chance to showcase my horsemanship and pride for this sport was fun.

"Try the white one. The red hat is too much," she shuddered. I swapped the matching red hat for a crisp white felt cowgirl hat that had a gorgeous tiara on the front. It slid over my teased hair like it was made for my head.

"Oh, I like this." I shot a look at Dixie, who was standing behind me in the large floor to ceiling mirror. The fact that Dixie's office is decked out like a changing room for royalty was icing on the cake.

"That's the one, honey." She beamed her perfect white teeth at me. "Now, let's think about the shoes."

*****

When Dixie and I had hammered out every little fine detail of my place in the pageant, I changed back into my diner uniform, which was so glitz and glam, I could wear it in a pageant. The blouse was mint green with paisley embroidery on the shoulders. The apron, wrapped around my waist, was a gorgeous denim that was covered in rhinestones that read *The Rodeo Cafe.* Per my uniform, the blouse was to be worn with bling jeans, tucked in, and a rhinestone belt. I was given a small allowance every six months to refresh my items. Dixie always said that presentation was everything.

We had a huge number of local customers who would dine with us every morning for breakfast, most of them retirees. Then, for lunch, we had a lot of working class. I didn't work very many evening shifts due to rodeo, but last time I did, there was a slew of regulars for that, too. Dixie was very well known and respected in Iron Spur, and I was blessed to work here and be under her wing.

As I stepped back out, I walked into a full-blown lunch rush. The sound of the clinking glasses and silverware hitting plates, paired with the smell of fresh coffee being brewed—Dixie never let it go stale—was a comfort to my senses. Most of the men donned cowboy hats, and almost everyone inside was wearing worn leather boots that sounded smooth on the tile floor.

Within moments, I was chatting with two ladies, who liked to come in every Friday for a piece of pie, when I overheard Dixie already sharing to half of the diner the details of my pageant dress. As she described the outfit from head to toe, glances were thrown my way of locals sizing me up to be their rodeo queen. I was met with warm smiles from everyone as the excitement of this new adventure really took hold in my mind.

Another group walked in, interrupting my thoughts, and I happily sat them in a booth. While I was retrieving their drinks, two Cokes, an iced tea, and a Dr. Pepper, the door chimed again.

"Hi, Liam!" Dixie exclaimed, the hope in her voice higher than it was when describing my rodeo queen aspirations.

"Hey, Dixie," he replied. As I poured the last of the drinks, I wondered why I couldn't bring myself to look over my shoulder. Surely, I could keep my finger on the button of this soda fountain and steal a glance his way. I set the cups on a tray, tossed a few straws down, and spun back around towards my new table. Towards Liam. Towards something else that was causing me an uncomfortable feeling.

Liam was holding a bouquet of flowers. I didn't know why, but I felt embarrassed by it. I felt like he shouldn't be here as often as he was. I felt like he was invading my space and messing with my head. Dixie didn't miss a beat, as the thoughts of her matchmaking not being as picture-perfect as she hoped flashed before her eyes.

"Savannah, look what Liam brought you," she said, as I was just finishing up taking the order from this new table. They knew what they wanted, which gave me the perfect excuse to delay my greeting towards Liam a little longer. Dixie knew I could listen to her and take an order, so she just had to chime in.

My table looked over at Liam on the cue of Dixie. "Isn't that just the sweetest!" one of the ladies called out. "Very gentlemanly," another said.

"Liam is Savannah's boyfriend," Dixie announced to another table, pointing back at Liam, who was now sitting in my section, of course. Then, it happened. A slip of words. Someone, somewhere in the cafe, said *his* name.

"...Colter." I turned my head fast. I couldn't figure out the source. No one was looking at me in that particular second. It was said under their breath. I may have been the only one to catch it. I drew a deep breath, pausing in the moment. All of these people had known me for most of my life. That meant they also knew about Colter. It wasn't a secret that we were head over heels in love. It wasn't a secret that he hadn't returned since.

Suddenly, the obligation to greet Liam was nagging at my mind. *Lord, please help me here. Is this the man you want for me? Everyone else thinks so. If so, help me get there, God.* My prayers were short lived, as I grabbed a pitcher of iced tea and made my way to his table. He stood and kissed me on the cheek. *Oohs and ahhs* could be heard ringing throughout the restaurant as now, my job was even more performative than usual.

"Good afternoon, Savannah," he said, handing me the beautiful bouquet of pink roses. They were stunning. Liam loved bringing me flowers. Just in the last week, I'd had to buy two more vases to fit them all.

"The ones you gave me two days ago are still alive and well. Now, they are going to be jealous of these." I smiled. "Thank you."

"All the flowers in the world can't compete with your beauty, Savannah." His words were smooth. So smooth, that I felt my heart flutter at his compliment. *Okay, God. Maybe You are telling me something here.*

"You are sweet." I breathed in the flowers one more time, before asking him if he was hungry. "I'm assuming you are also here to have lunch?" I asked, to which he nodded.

"Who's cookin' today?" he asked, playfully peering back to see the man in the kitchen.

"It's Freddie on Friday's," I smiled. Freddie was known for his fried chicken, which had a following of its own.

"In that case, tell him I'll take whatever he can whip me up." With a handsome smile, he squeezed my hand. I was never more aware of the fact that half of the diner had their eyes on me, just out of curiosity if anything, so I smiled and winked at him, something I would have never done otherwise. Again, the uncomfortable feeling returned.

Suddenly, the dishwasher Jimmy appeared again with a vase in hand. It was filled up halfway with water. "Want me to take those and put them in here?" he asked, pointing at my bouquet.

"Sure," I laughed, handing him the flowers.

"And Freddie has got your chicken comin' right up, man." Jimmy walked away. Every bone in my body wanted the eyes of the cafe to get off of me. I wished for anyone to walk through the door, so I had a reason to walk away. Finally, a customer named Gary held up his coffee cup to me, a gesture meaning he wanted a refill.

"Gotta go," I said, as I took off, making it my life mission to refill the cup of Joe as fast as I could.

"Thanks, Savannah," Gary said. He was in his late 80's, and he and his wife Lorna used to sponsor the peewee rodeo sports when I was little. I absolutely loved them.

"You're welcome. Say, I think there's a big slice of huckleberry pie left. If only I could pawn it off on someone, we could replace it in the case with something else." I crossed my arms and tapped my finger on my chin.

"You know a sucker when you see one," he grinned. "Extra whipped cream, please." After piling the whipped cream as high as it would go without toppling over, I returned the plate to Gary. "That looks like more than one slice. Good thing I got my sweetheart here with me." Lorna's eyes were wide at the generous dessert.

"You two kids enjoy it," I said, dropping off two fresh forks.

"Savannah," Gary said, taking a bite of the huckleberries, "I saw you and Liam." His tone was low, and I was confident that the rest of the diner had turned their attention back onto their food.

"Yes, we're dating now," I said with a shy smile. Gary nodded.

"It surprised me," he shrugged.

"Oh? Why is that?" I was whispering back as quietly as I could. The two large hearing aids in his ears let me know he didn't miss a beat.

"The contrast between you and Liam, and you with..." He trailed off as Lorna elbowed him. I knew what he meant.

"Gary..." I trailed off, looking for the words to say. I didn't have to prove anything to anyone. I, too, was struggling with this same thing. "He's been gone for five years." I felt like my statements were more like a question, as if I was taking a poll of everyone else's expectation of my love life. The boy I had met when I was 16? Well, now I was 21. I'd changed, too.

"Forgive Gary," Lorna interjected. "The Lord has the greatest plan for your life, and maybe it is Liam. He's a great kid from a wonderful family." Hearing Lorna echo Dixie's speech made my stomach twist. Yes, he was from a great family. I felt God nudge my heart at this very moment, but for what, I hadn't realized yet.

"Enjoy your pie," I said, spinning around on my heels and heading back to Liam with a smile. Something about saying the words out loud, that Colter was gone, made me look at Liam with renewed eyes.

CHAPTER 9
AND THE ROCKET'S RED GLARE

Savannah

"Howdy, gorgeous," Liam said, working his best cowboy drawl. But we both knew he wasn't a cowboy. He didn't care for horses. He didn't ranch. Sure, his family had sizable sugar beet crops, and they ran a farm and ranch store, but that was as close as he got to being western. His job was spent in an office all day doing IT, for crying out loud. But Liam had been coming to the rodeo for several weeks now, watching me compete, and at the most recent event, he wore a cowboy hat.

I almost laughed at first. It wasn't that I was teasing him or making fun of him in any way; I just wasn't expecting it. He looked good in the hat; there was no denying that. If I hadn't known him, I wouldn't have given it another thought beyond that he looked hot. But I did know him. I knew that his life was spent working on fiber optics and faulty internet connections. He was in charge of websites and phone lines. He held up the operation of his family's store and the surrounding businesses who needed his help, absolutely, but he wasn't a cowboy.

When Colter was 17, he could lift a 400-lb. hay bale. Wyoming men were built different. Most of them, anyway. Liam, while he was tall and muscular—I wouldn't expect him to be able to lift half of that. I felt God nudge my heart again. Maybe I needed to stop comparing the stark differences between these two men? After all, Liam was here in front of me.

Liam started chatting to me about his afternoon job he was heading to. The town of Iron Spur had some technical problem with this year's drones they were using for the fireworks show that he had been consulting on.

"For some reason, whenever it casts a cowboy hat, a boot shows up next to it. Something faulty in the programming." He bored on while I started to glaze over.

"Is that really a bad thing, though? What's wrong with a boot next to a cowboy hat? They go together, I'd think." He shook his head.

"They might go together in theory," he said, taking a sip of his iced tea, "but in reality, they are two separate things entirely. They each need their own chance to dazzle across the sky by themselves." My heart was nudged once more, but I still didn't know why.

Liam left after lunch. The rest of my shift was lackluster as I started daydreaming about barrel racing. My desire to ride Daisy as fast as I could around three barrels was overwhelming. So, after my shift ended, that's just what I announced I'd do.

"I'm headed to the arena. See you tomorrow?" I asked Dixie, who had a list of things we needed to work out before my entry into the pageant next month.

"No," she shook her head. "The fireworks planning committee needs to meet with everyone from the Iron Spur Rodeo Association to plan out the show for the 4th. If you thought we were patriotic here in Iron Spur, wait until you see the 250th birthday of America!" Her excitement was contagious, and I felt giddy just hearing about it.

As I drove to the arena at my parents' ranch, I beamed at the beautiful sights on my way there. Fresh flags had just been put out, lining the streets of downtown. Red, white, and blue tinsel stars were sparkling on every corner. Someone was walking down a side street holding a bouquet of silver balloons that the sun glared off of, nearly blinding everyone in their path.

There were few things I loved more than the 4th of July in Iron Spur; like I always said, Jesus and the Fourth of July, in that order. The festivities alone were the heartbeat of our town. The fireworks. The songs. The parades—we had one every day of the week before the 4th. People finally pulled out their summer cars that they kept garaged until the threat of lousy weather was officially gone. Shiny pickup trucks and vintage cars cruising the main street was a common sight. It wasn't uncommon to see bull horns attached to the front end of a vehicle. The rodeo car that would often drive around Iron Spur's rodeo queen had a megaphone attached to it that would invite everyone out to the rodeo, which was seven nights a week. The buzz and excitement felt as electric as the horses' hooves clicking on the pavement during the daily parades the week of the 4th. Iron Spur was my favorite place to be.

Daisy and I practiced well into the evening. As the sun began to set, I watched it from the saddle of my most faithful companion, as I ran my fingers through her mane. Something was changing in me. Today, I saw Liam differently. I felt comfortable in my relationship with him. I enjoyed how beautiful he made me feel. I was starting to feel... happy again. As I watched the sun dip below the horizon, I felt a change in the air. The wind shifted ever so slightly, and it was now blowing in a direction that didn't often happen in the summer. In all my time spent growing up on this ranch, the only time the wind had blown from that direction was when a powerful storm was moving over a ridge in our valley. Tonight, the skies were clear, but something was coming. I could feel it.

CHAPTER 10
THE BOMB BURSTING IN AIR

Savannah

"The fourth of July is just a few days away, Savannah. If you want to end the night with a crown on your hat, we need to get this down." Dixie went through all of the points for my horsemanship presentation that I'd be giving at the pageant next week. The nerves hadn't hit me yet; I'd never done any form of public speaking before. While I had performed in barrel racing in front of crowds, the thought of talking in front of them made me feel weak in the knees.

Later, as we reviewed my speech on what rodeo meant to me, she started throwing questions at me that the judges might ask. Finally, we started to wrap up. It was almost time for my lunch shift, and I'd been here since eight in the morning to prepare for the pageant.

"Just a second, Savannah," Dixie said with a wink. Her glittery bangles clinging together, and she swayed over to the corner of her huge office and picked up a few shopping bags. "This is the fun part." She pulled out a new pair of gorgeous Miss Me jeans with glittering horseshoes and bejeweled flaps on the back pockets. A sparkling silver belt followed, with a gorgeous, white, embroidered western button up shirt. It had a small filigree of hot pink flowers and paisley around the chest and cuffs of the arms. In the final bag, she pulled out a cowgirl hat that had sparkling stars under the brim that were visible when I turned my head. I felt like rodeo royalty just looking at it.

"I'm blown away, Dixie." I reached out and hugged her. "Your generosity is just too much," I said, squeezing her tightly. "I love everything, and I can't wait to wear it."

"Now, now, sweetheart. I'm your sponsor for the pageant. This is my duty to get you the outfits, remember?" I pulled out of the hug, and she winked at me.

"You have much better taste than the other sponsors." I thought back to last year's pageant, and I didn't remember a single contestant who had a western wear outfit that was this cute.

"Stick with me, Savannah, and you'll always be sparkling." She winked, and I caught a glimpse of her sparkling eyeshadow that glittered on her lids.

*****

When we were finished, I changed into my diner uniform behind her dressing shade.

"I forgot to bring a hair tie," I said, pulling my strawberry blonde locks back with my hand. Dixie handed me an oversized hair clip that looked like it was from Liberace's personal collection. I smiled and rolled my eyes. Dixie didn't do anything halfway, ever, and I'd bet money that even her socks had sparkles on them.

Quickly in the large mirror, I dabbed a little blush on my freckled cheeks and applied a quick coat of mascara on my blonde eyelashes. The red lipstick Dixie bought for the pageant was just sitting there, so I figured I'd give that a test run, too. I didn't always wear makeup, but after working on my "glam" for the last several hours, I just felt like it. I guess I was in the mood to be dramatic today.

A few small pieces of my hair slipped out of the clip, falling onto my face. I didn't have time to play with my hair all day, as I could already hear the door chiming with customers arriving for lunch.

"See you out there," I said to Dixie with a smile as she waved me off, doing one final look at all of my outfits as she slipped them on mannequin busts and taking notes on her clipboard.

Stepping out onto the diner floor, I assessed the tables. Three groups had already arrived, plus one table with a single person. From the back of the man, I could tell it was Liam. I smiled and grabbed a stack of menus to pass out. When I finally reached him, I had already taken two orders and more hair slipped out of the clip.

"Good afternoon, *darling.*" My greeting was extra flamboyant, as I'd just gotten two compliments on my lipstick. I was full of it. But immediately, I noticed Liam didn't react. He was staring off into space. Something was very, very wrong. I slid into the booth in front of him. "What's up?" He shook his head.

"Nothing, just a little stressed today. It will be fine," he said, finally looking at me. His eyes opened wider when he did. "Wow, you look *extra* gorgeous today." He reached over the table and took my hand in his. I gave his hands a squeeze.

"Thank you. Well, I better go put these orders in," I said. Now that I knew he was okay, I needed to get back to work.

"And I'll do whatever Freddie wants to make today," he said, not looking at the menu.

"Freddie only works Fridays, remember?" Today was Monday.

"Oh, that's right. In that case, uhm," Liam quickly scoured the menu.

"How about the French dip? You like that." He nodded.

"Yeah, that sounds good." My concern for Liam was coming back. This wasn't his usual behavior. His doting, kind-hearted personality was missing today. And I didn't need them, and I was certainly not expecting them, but he usually brought me flowers when he came in, so the absence of them was noticeable.

After putting in all of the orders, the door chimed again. I was just refilling a pitcher of iced tea to deliver to one of the groups at table two when the room went quiet. I felt the air in the room shift, thinking how the warm breeze outside must have stopped. It felt stuffy in here as I readjusted my collar. If I didn't know any better, I would have said the soft country music that was playing was muted, but we'd been having issues with our sound system. Actually, Dixie was going to ask Liam to fix that for her next time she saw him. Probably today. Just then, Dixie walked out of her office and over to me. She was holding a stack of fabric swatches, most likely trying to gauge a color for something for the pageant. But Dixie froze.

"I like that second red one," I said, turning off the iced tea spigot. "Can someone turn the air back on? It's warm in here," I asked, and Dixie looked back with wide eyes to Jimmy in the kitchen who was fumbling with a stack of dishes. The pitcher now filled, I spun around and proceeded to drop the pitcher from my hand, it's contents spilling all over the floor. Not that I saw it. My shoes felt wet from the liquid. My ankles cold from the ice. I never saw anything past *him.*

It was his shoulders first. Broad, like they were holding up the weight of the world. His unmistakable boots next—why my eyes went down like I couldn't let myself see his face yet. Brown, broken in, ostrich leather, with steel-toe tips. Custom made, no other pair like it around here that I'd noticed. My eyes looked away at the mess on the floor, and they filled up with tears. My pulse was through the roof. I needed another paper bag to breathe in. The room was feeling fuzzy. He stepped toward me.

"Savannah." The words from Colter's lips meant this was real. I wasn't dreaming of this. It wasn't a mirage. I finally gave in and took in his perfect face. He had grown up. He looked older. Tougher. Like he had been through a war. His jawline was more pronounced. Everything about him looked more muscular, even his neck. His hair wasn't shaggy anymore.—for someone who was in the military, that made sense. Still, the absence of his signature hairstyle startled me. Then again, I knew Colter could grow a head of hair in a few months. His whole family was that way. I hadn't let myself think of them in ages.

I put my hands on the pie counter like I was trying to summon the strength to win a pie eating contest. My head bowed and my forehead leaned on the glass of the case; feeling its cooling calmed me down. This was happening. Colter was here. Colter was back in Iron Spur, and he was feet away from me, calling my name, but I was too weak to answer, as the world went dark.

CHAPTER 11

GAVE PROOF THROUGH THE NIGHT

Colter

I knew this was a bad idea. Coming into the diner wasn't the ideal space to be reunited with the woman I hadn't been able to stop thinking about for the last five years, but when I saw her rickety, old truck parked out back, I couldn't help myself.

I'd been back in town for about two seconds. I had just driven through the night to get here. Barely greeting my parents, who I'd only seen over video calls in the last several years, before leaving again. Then, I pulled in to get some fuel.

The leather of my wallet was so worn in the creases, I thought it might fall apart every time I opened it up, similar to how I felt. Inside was a picture of Savannah that I had from our last night together. She was sitting on the horse wearing all of the sparkling tinsel and regalia that Iron Spur brought for the

Fourth of July. It was the photo that I kept in my chest pocket every day since I left. Only when I was honorably discharged three days ago did the photo go into my wallet. After paying at the pump, I closed my wallet and put it back in my pocket.

Fueling up at the pump on the other side of mine was a guy I had known from church growing up. I didn't know him at first, but there was something about his whistling that made me remember. The guy was reciting a tune so joyfully, as if it was the best day of his life. Like he had just returned from half a world away. Like he had spent the last five years of his life thinking at any moment, he might die and never get to see the love of his life again, and now he was back, in one piece. I guess you could say I resonated with the feeling. So, I looked around the pump, and my face met his.

"Liam." I held my hand out to shake his, and his whistling immediately stopped. The tapping of his foot stopped. The only audible noise between us was the fuel going through the lines and into our trucks. A solemn expression was cast as he reached his hand out, slowly, like I might have a buzzer on my palm. Then it hit me: *He didn't recognize me.*

"Colter Hays, remember? We went to church together for a year or two, until I turned 18 and joined the Army," I smirked, pretending the words didn't hurt when they came out. Pretending I hadn't missed every moment that I had been away. As if every second without Savannah didn't feel like a burning in my lungs.

Liam didn't respond, but he stared at me with a fierce intensity after shaking my hand.

"Alright, then." I pulled my hand away and turned back to the pump, the dog tags around my neck sitting like an anchor on my body. The weight of them suddenly became known to me. In this setting, they felt foreign. *Heavy.* The fuel pump clicked, letting me know my truck was full. I unhooked it and climbed back into the truck, my hands shaking as I gripped the set of keys about to turn over in the ignition. *Now what, Lord?* I prayed for my next steps, but the truck was already in motion, driving down the streets I knew like the back of my hand. This was the same week I left all of those years ago, and Iron Spur was still decorated the same. Nothing much had changed, except maybe some freshly painted signs and new bunting to replace the sun-faded ones of the past.

For a moment, I pretended that I had never left. That God had given me a second chance at my life. That I was 18 again and did not have to go off and witness the horrors of battle—the emotional, jarring nature of war. That I didn't have to leave my home, my family, and the girl I fell in love with. Now, Savannah was twenty-one years old. I let that settle in for a moment and for a second, I wondered if she was still here? The panic of it made me uneasy. What if she had moved away? I would go there. If she'd moved on? I would respect that. If she was not interested in seeing me? I wasn't prepared for that reality. As I took a turn, got on the main drag of Iron Spur, and drove around to the back of the Rodeo Diner, I saw her truck parked and my body was filled with an undeniable magnetism that controlled the rest of my movements.

Walking in the front door, two patrons were leaving. One woman gave me a double take and froze before looking back at the door. Like she was considering going back inside. As if she knew what was about to go down, and she wanted to see it firsthand. The other diner, a man, put his arm around her and guided her to their car.

My hand gripped the sunbaked metal handle of the door, and I stepped inside. It was darker in the diner than it was outside, so my eyes took a moment to adjust, but when they did, I saw her immediately. She had her back to me. Her hair was different—longer, maybe, still light from the sun like it was that last summer I was here. She seemed taller, a confident arch to her back. It took all of the self-control God gave me at this moment to not just go wrap my arms around her.

Dixie walked out, and we immediately made eye contact. A mix of emotions crossed her face, and none of which seem pleased to see me. Someone turned off the quiet music, maybe so that they could see better? I heard Savannah's voice; it was the tone that I imagined the angels in heaven would sing in. It instantly grounded me. It erased the things I'd seen since. It erased the things I'd felt. The heaviest pack I'd carried in the last five years was loneliness, and now, in this moment, it had been lifted.

Then, because God was a God of miracles, Savannah turned around, and I saw her. I looked into her eyes. I took in the unbelievable beauty of her face, and though I still saw her as a sixteen-year-old girl on the sparkling horse, she was standing before me as a grown woman. Her lips were painted in my favorite color of red. Two blonde swaths of her hair were freed from the giant sparkling clip that was holding them back. It all happened so fast that I didn't get to say anything before she dropped the pitcher she was holding in her hand. The iced tea went everywhere, flooding out the back area of the diner where she was standing. It almost reached my feet, when she started to look like she might faint, and then she started to go down. Dixie caught her, but the weight of Savannah being slumped in her arms couldn't be easy on her. I stepped in, offering to carry her somewhere, when Dixie looked behind me. She was staring at someone, and I turned to look, seeing Liam again. It all made sense now.

Dixie ultimately nodded, telling me to carry Savannah to her office couch, where she was one step in front of me, opening the door and turning the fan on full blast. After I laid her on the brightly colored leather couch, I hesitated, turning back to Dixie.

"So," she said, crossing her arms. I looked down at my feet.

"So," I said back.

"What does this all mean, Colter? Are you back? Or did you just come back because you sensed she was finally getting her life back on track after several years of it being derailed by your breaking up with her?" The guilt washed over me like I'd been lowered into a pool.

"I guess I…" I trailed off, only now realizing that I had no idea. Other than being honorably discharged from the Army,

I had no idea what was next. I was living between two worlds—
the life of a soldier and the memory of here. Of her. Dixie saw
right through me, as she saw right through everyone she ever
looked at. My parents used to say you didn't even need to tell
Dixie what you were thinking; you just needed to stand next to
her, and she knew. Her perception levels were off the charts,
and I was relying on them in this very moment where I lacked
the words to speak or the ideas for my life because I'd never felt
so lost as I did right now. Standing near Savannah, I'd also never
felt so found.

Dixie uncrossed her arms and leaned in to hug me.
Relief came to me in a second wave.

"She missed you more than anything," Dixie offered,
while we were in a deep hug. I felt tears behind my eyes come.
I hadn't cried since I was a kid. The water works were here. A
small tear escaped the corner of my eye when Dixie released me
from the hug. With her long fingers with painted nails that
matched the couch, she wiped it away. "Why don't you go sit in
that back booth, and I'll bring you a piece of my famous cherry
pie, while we wait for her to come to?" I nodded, feeling relieved
that she was allowing me to stay. Wanting to ask more questions
about what Dixie meant when she said that Savannah was finally

back on track. Not wanting to know what Liam had to do with any of it.

When I walked back out to the front of the diner, the music was still off. All eyes were looking at me with shock. Awe. Wonder. I looked to the right of the room, and Liam had left. I slid into the booth, facing the front door, and my rear hadn't been touching the seat for fifteen seconds before people started to break their silence and finally go back to their meals and conversations. I let out a breath of relief.

Jimmy, Dixie's right-hand man in the diner, came out to me and shook my hand.

"Thank you for your service, Colter." He grinned ear to ear and had my hand in both of his. I nodded back, a flashback of walking through the desert sands in a particularly dangerous situation appearing in my mind. A burst of anxiety tearing through me, I said a silent prayer to God for my strength to overcome these feelings. My hands were shaking as Jimmy let go. "I'm going to get you a fresh glass of iced tea," he said, as he walked away.

Moments later, Dixie emerged with a slice of pie so big, it didn't fit on the small plate, with a bowl of whipped cream next to it. "I couldn't remember if you liked a little or a lot." She motioned to the bowl, but everyone in Iron Spur loved Dixie's pie with a heaping helping of whipped cream, and I was no different in that regard.

I picked up the metal fork but felt the weight of a plastic utensil I ate my MRE's with in the desert. Putting the pie to my mouth, the sugary sweetness filling my senses before I even took a bite, my mouth watered as I bit into the glorious treat, with its hints of cinnamon and pineapple enticing memories. Memories of that last summer. Memories of the last night here in Iron Spur, where I made promises to Savannah I didn't know if I could keep.

CHAPTER 12
THAT OUR FLAG WAS STILL THERE

Savannah

"Savannah?" I opened my eyes, and Dixie was standing above where I lay on her hot pink leather tooled couch in her office. The ceiling fan was on full blast, rocking back and forth as it oscillated above me. My eyes focused on it, as I wondered if it might fall on me. If it did, I wouldn't have to face Colter. Remembering that he was here, I shot up from the couch. Unless it was all a dream?

"Did *he* come in?" I couldn't say his name aloud. I needed strength just to ask that question. Dixie looked away, going back to the busts wearing my pageant outfits.

"Yes, he did." My heart skipped a beat.

"And is he... still here?" I asked, paying no mind to the fact that I was missing part of my memory of this afternoon.

"He is. You fainted. He carried you to this couch. Liam left, however." The uncertainty in Dixie's voice was palpable. *Liam.* In the hustle and bustle, he wasn't even remotely near the top of my mind. I didn't know what to do in this situation, and I didn't think Dixie did, either.

"I'm sorry, Dixie, but I don't feel so well. I need to go home," I said, wearily. In all of my years working here, I'd never once flaked out on her during a shift like this. She nodded, bringing over a digital thermometer and holding it up to my head.

"You almost have a fever, but it's sweltering in here," she said, while holding a cool, wet washcloth to my forehead. "You should go. I'll be fine here. I can always call in Katelyn." Katelyn worked a few days a month for the diner, the most part-time a person could get while still technically maintaining employment, as she was in school year-round for nursing. But this close to the 4th of July, the diner might as well have been the only business open, so we knew the school was closed, too. The town of Iron Spur was expected to halt all activities it could so that everyone could partake in its annual festivities, after all.

"Thank you. I'll see you tomorrow." I got up, holding the washcloth to my face and using it to wipe the sweat off of my hairline, as I went to the mirror. My cute hairstyle was still present, just a little messed up. My lipstick hadn't smeared, but my mascara was dangerously close. I felt emotion building up inside as I struggled to put one foot in front of the other, like I was walking through mud.

Leaving Dixie's office, I didn't know whether to escape out the back door and slip into my truck or walk through the front of the diner and face Colter. If he was even out there. The diner, in many ways, was my safe space, but for this, I thought the situation was much more delicate, and I sought a more private setting. I stopped in the kitchen and asked Jimmy to pass along a message to Colter that I would meet him at my truck in the parking lot. Jimmy quickly agreed, always wanting to get right in the middle of a situation, and I went out the back door, not turning around once to see Colter. Not yet.

When I reached my truck, the sun was beating down in the heat of the day. Marching bands could be heard out on the street out front, blowing into their tubas and flutes with all they had. A fast drum rhythm met my heartbeat. I climbed into the hot truck, quickly rolling down the windows. The leather seats were scalding and sticking to the backs of my arms. I paid no attention to the heat. I couldn't focus on the third-degree burns

I was feeling on any exposed skin that was touching it. All I could do was wait for the man I'd been waiting on for five years to emerge.

A few seconds later, Colter walked around the back of the diner building to the employee lot where I was sitting, his eyes cast downward. Like he was holding onto shame. Like he wasn't ready to look me in the eye after leaving and breaking things off with me all those years ago. It wasn't until he made it to the passenger side of my truck that he stopped and stalled.

"May I join you?" His voice was deeper than it was, stronger, and sounded like he only used it now when he spoke intentionally. My voice was dry. I tried to speak, but no words came out. After a long hesitation, where I stared at the man who both looked so different, but still the same, I nodded. He climbed into the sweltering truck. It didn't have air conditioning. The only way we could cool down was if we went for a drive. But the marching bands were just getting going for the day, and traffic would be blocked off for at least an hour while they paraded through the streets of Iron Spur. Besides, I didn't know if I could think clearly enough to operate heavy machinery right now. I'd just woken up from fainting, after all.

"Do you want to go somewhere with me?" Colter asked, breaking the painful silence between us. The silence that carried so much weight of things I wanted to say. Things I wanted to ask. But at the same time, Colter felt like a stranger to me. This felt like a fever dream. I remembered Dixie saying I *almost* had a fever, after all. Perhaps this was all in my head, and I imagined all of it. I reached out and touched his hand. I still couldn't speak. His hand felt very real. Very rough. I had memorized the intricacies of his hands when he was here before, how my hand felt in his palm. How my fingers fit around his. Now, these hands looked like those of a stranger with their callouses. With their new strength. That's how I knew this was real. If this was a dream, they wouldn't look like they'd been through a war. I couldn't make this up.

"Okay," I whispered, agreeing to his question after several minutes, as I still studied the feel of his hand. Colter sat while I did so, his presence bringing me the intensity of emotions I'd been missing since he left. The powerful longing. The deep-rooted feeling of love. Like this was the man whom God had always had for me.

Thoughts of Liam crossed my mind again, and I slowly pulled my hand away, as I revealed a loaded truth.

"I have a boyfriend." The words carried a pain behind them. Colter slowly nodded, putting his hand on the door handle like he was about to leave me. Again. "Wait," I said, suddenly feeling like I was pleading with him. "We can still have a conversation. We can still catch up and respect the boundaries." Deep down, I knew that I was willing to drop any man like a hot potato for Colter, but I still didn't know what this was even about. I didn't know what Colter was about or why he was back now. For how long he was back. Though now that I'd seen him, I knew that I could never love Liam the way he deserved because my heart was reserved for the soldier beside me.

Colter didn't leave the truck, but he didn't say anything, either. We sat in the silence between us that felt raw, unbearable, yet calming to my spirit. Just having him near me was like filling the hole in my heart that had been empty ever since.

Finally, the marching band could be heard making their final song, the *Star-Spangled Banner*. Everyone in Iron Spur would be out lining the streets with their hands over their hearts right now. Just hearing it made my love for the country run through my veins. Just hearing the song made me tear up a little. I glanced at Colter, the man who was once just a boy telling me how much he disliked the Fourth of July. How much he disliked all of the parades and activities because it reminded him what was in store for his future. The country he loved enough to protect, but the inevitable risk of death that he faced in exchange. I wondered now how he felt that he'd made it through. He'd made it back home. Back to the girl that had just told him she has a boyfriend. Back to the girl that he ended things with all those years ago.

Colter stiffened up as the music ended, while a cool breeze finally picked up and blew through my open truck windows.

"I better go," I said to Colter, ending this so he didn't have to. After all, he was ready to leave when I broke the news of my dating someone else. While he didn't know the details of this brand-new relationship—the one that everyone encouraged me to jump into to get my mind finally off of the man that had now galivanted back into my life—I realized I needed some time before I decided what to do. I needed some reflection. I needed some clarification. As if on cue, Colter spoke.

"I'm not going anywhere, Savannah. I'm back in Iron Spur to stay." My heart leapt like it was trying out for acrobatics in the Olympics. He slid off of the leather bucket seats, stepped out onto the worn concrete of the employee parking lot, and left while I watched him walk away. Back into his old truck that reminded me of everything I ever wanted. Back down main street, that I could barely see, but the sliver I could looked just like the last time he was here.

Seeing him now, all of these years later, reminded me that when he first left, I never would have imagined he would be gone for that long. Soldiers got to come home sometimes, right? They got leave. They got to contact family. They got phone calls. I had nothing but a few short letters, each one colder than the last, and an unresolved breakup.

The more I let myself dwell on the past, the more came flooding back to me, and the more I was left questioning everything. The only thing I knew now was that I needed to talk to Liam.

CHAPTER 13

O SAY DOES THAT STAR-SPANGLED BANNER YET WAVE

Savannah

I went straight home after work, walked into my apartment that overlooked the rodeo grounds, and turned on my window air conditioner full blast, as I methodically thumbed through my closet to find the perfect shirt to wear tonight, my mind not processing what had just gone down. I was barrel racing at 8:30 p.m., and leaving my shift hours early gave me more time than usual to prepare. But normally, I didn't have to prepare. I just went in and did the ride. Now, everything had changed.

A cold shower might have been the only thing that would cool me off after nearly getting heat stroke in my hot pickup truck where I had just sat with Colter in silence all afternoon. The words he said to me kept playing on repeat in my head—that he was not going anywhere. That he was here to stay. Turning on the faucet, I cranked the water to as icy as it got, but it still felt lukewarm on my flushed skin. There, I stood letting the water wash over me and praying to God for guidance. I imagined the cool water being poured from His hands and rinsing me clean of the pain I'd been living in all this time. The longer I stood there in prayer, I started to cool off. I reconnected with God. He reminded me that I was not walking this path alone, and the Holy Spirit filled me with peace.

Later that afternoon, I drove out to my parents' house to get Daisy. We still had a few hours until we needed to report to the contestants stand at the rodeo, and the scents coming from the kitchen were irresistible.

"Tell me you are making rosemary crackers?" I asked, poking my head inside of the house. My mother was a little quieter than usual and just nodded. My interest peaked, and I kicked off my boots that were covered in dirt from the rodeo and stepped inside. "Everything okay, Mom?" I asked. She looked at me with a concerned look.

"I was going to ask you the same thing, Savannah." She pulled a towel off of a dough bowl and threw it on her left shoulder. I watched her wash her hands and considered what she meant while she stood wringing them on her apron. She must have known about Colter.

"You heard? Already? Did a carrier pigeon fly out and deliver a scroll with the information?" She shook her head.

"Billy tried to burn ditches today, but he called in for a burn permit for the first time. Apparently, Colter's mom wasn't working dispatch today, and Billy asked why. Her substitute told him the news that Colter had just gotten home from the Army, after being away for five years..." She trailed off. A lump formed in my throat. Her eyes were watering as she spoke. My mother loved Colter when we were together. So did my dad. They mourned with me when he left. Cried with me when he broke things off. I wasn't the only one bracing myself for what his return could mean. Now, as I stood in her farmhouse kitchen, I felt my knees go weak. I felt the tears bringing a hundred of their closest friends. I felt all of the strength I was pretending to have the last five years dissolve in an instant.

"I don't know what to do," I said, as I kicked off my breakdown. It wasn't all sadness—I would be a liar if I said I didn't feel joy that he was back. Relief. Seeing him again made me feel like he was my walking second chance. I told her everything that had happened. I shared my feelings, ones I hadn't even explored yet myself, and then my guilt about Liam. It was clear to me that I needed to break up with him, regardless, because I just didn't have the feelings for him that I should for the person I dated.

"Liam sounds like a really nice guy," my mom said, her voice filled with regret. "But dating is for marriage, and if you don't see yourself marrying Liam…" She trailed off.

"No," I said quickly, shaking my head. Sure, I had fun with him, but marriage was out of the question. At this point, if I took it any further, I was just leading him on.

"So, that's settled then." She smiled for the first time since I walked in, and I, too, felt better. The round timer on her oven dinged, as the scent of rosemary sea salt crackers wafted through my senses. "Are you staying for dinner?" she asked, while her back was to me, checking a large pot that had been simmering on the stove. "I've made homemade tomato soup, with tomatoes fresh from the garden this morning."

"Twist my arm," I said, pulling a chair out from the kitchen table. My breakdown having passed, I actually felt better after crying about it. If anything, it was healing to let it all out.

As she served me a bowl of soup, with a side of her specialty almond flour crackers fresh from the oven and a thickly-sliced grilled cheese on sourdough bread, she didn't ask what I was going to do about Colter. But she spoke as if things were settled by his return. Like life would now go on, as it should have all along.

My dad eventually putted into the dining room, giving me a quick hug before sitting down. My mom gave him a look, like after all of these years together they could speak telepathically, and he nodded, smiling. They were both smiling. There was a relaxation to their postures. There was an ease that felt both foreign and familiar, like Colter's hands, that had also made a re-entry to life this afternoon. I was thankful for it all but still wracked with anxiety about ending things with Liam. I had never broken up with anyone before. I never intended to hurt anyone. I had never intended to date anyone who wasn't Colter and yet, just a month before he returned, I got myself into this situation. I prayed to God He would help me out of it now.

After dinner, I went to hook up my horse trailer, and my dad volunteered to help. "Are you coming tonight to the rodeo?" I asked him, and he nodded.

"We wouldn't miss the nightly rodeo for the world." I knew they loved watching it, whether I was in it or not. We were a rodeo family, living in a rodeo town, and experiencing the events that the summer rodeo brings felt like we were living the most patriotic life we could. Honoring God with the opening prayer over the contestants. Honoring our military with the national anthem and every man, woman, and child with their hands over their hearts. And most importantly, honoring the freedom that was given to us by this great nation and doing the best that we could every day for it.

"I'll see you there." I leaned in and gave him a hug, as Daisy walked into the trailer.

*****

I arrived fifteen minutes earlier than the contestants were supposed to, but I used the time to prepare mentally for any questions people might throw at me. If my parents already knew about Colter, then it was more likely that Elvis himself would be entering the contestant chute tonight than it was likely that the entire crowd didn't know. Sure, maybe there were a handful of tourists here that wouldn't know by the sound of my name on the loudspeakers that I was now in some weird love triangle after a reunion at the Rodeo Diner.

After I got Daisy out of the horse trailer, I saw a familiar truck pull around back in the contestant only area. A truck that looked so out of place back here, it took me a moment to register that it was Liam. He parked, stepped out, and my heart skipped a beat with anticipation for what was to come as he walked over to me. I noticed his empty hands as he did. I felt relieved that he didn't bring flowers, because I didn't deserve flowers from this man. I didn't deserve to enjoy his company. I didn't deserve any of his time when I had no intention of staying with him. I was preparing my speech to deliver the blow as softly as possible while he walked over to me.

"Savannah," Liam said, with a depth to his voice I'd not heard before.

"Hi," I said, my voice quivering with nerves.

"Do you have a minute?" His eyes glazed over as he looked past me to Daisy. Despite living here, he almost looked uncomfortable around horses.

"Sure," I said, stammering. I was early, after all, but this felt like it wasn't going to go how I wanted it to.

"Thanks," Liam said, running his fingers through his curly blonde hair. "I just want to say that I have really loved getting to know you these last few weeks." My heart sank. What was this? "And I'm going to miss our dates." My jaw dropped. Liam was breaking up with *me.*

"Liam?" I asked in my confusion. He looked off in a blank stare back at Daisy and shook his head. I felt emotion welling up inside of me, and I didn't expect it. All of this was catching me totally off guard. I should have been happy. Honestly, I felt relieved. But that didn't mean I didn't care about the sweet guy standing in front of me, and right now, it was clear that he was hurting.

"I just want you to be happy, Savannah. However, that looks—" he shrugged his shoulders. The aviators blocked his eyes from me. I wish I could have looked at him, in his beautiful blue eyes, and told him I'd always care for him. That I'd never forget the fun nights we had, and I'd always appreciate the way he made me feel. But for some reason, my mind went in the opposite direction.

"Just because he's back, doesn't mean we are automatically together, you know." I don't know why I said it, but the words came out more in my own personal defense of how it looked, having me faint at the sight of my ex-boyfriend while trying to serve my current boyfriend lunch. How it made me feel that I had only just started seeing him when Colter returned. How it made me look that I wasn't ever sure about the relationship with Liam to begin with, and now, I looked like I was torn between two men, but really, my heart was always Colter's.

"You were never mine, Savannah." Liam shook his head as he spoke. "I prayed one day you would be, but I knew from the moment I saw Colter roll into town that we were in trouble. Then, I saw the way you looked at him. I just hope that one day I can find a woman so in love with me that she faints at the sight of this." He motioned to his body and laughed. I nodded when I realized that was why he was acting so strangely at the diner this morning; he had seen Colter before I did. He knew what was coming. And here we were.

Liam was right about everything. I was never his. I had never moved on from this past relationship. I'd never gotten over it, despite the encouragement of everyone around me. I've never felt even a hint of interest in dating anyone else. This was a fluke. A one-off, sporadic occurrence due to Dixie's meddling and Liam's persistence. All I could do in this moment was give him a hug, and that's what I did.

"Thank you for your kindness," I said to Liam as he pulled away, walking back to his truck. I got a sense that this might have been the last time I saw Liam for a while. I turned back to Daisy and gave her a carrot.

CHAPTER 14
O'ER THE LAND OF THE FREE

Savannah

The Fourth of July

"Don't forget the belt buckle," Dixie smiled, as she pulled out a giant piece of silver so polished that if direct sunlight hit it, it might have started a spontaneous fire. I nodded, as I started attaching the buckle to my belt that was covered in rhinestones. On the buckle was a rodeo image. It was from a famous Wyoming silversmith, Tom Barnes, according to the stamp on the back of it. Worth a pretty penny, too.

"Where did you find this?" I asked her, marveling at the sight, as I pulled the belt through the loops on my jeans.

"I know someone in the biz," Dixie winked.

"You have all the best connections," I told her. She shrugged knowingly.

"His daughter asked me to mentor her one summer when she was running for the Dust Creek rodeo queen. Tom knows how important this pageant is, and he's willing to send things out on loan every once in a while." Dixie clapped her hands together. Her long nails today were painted red, the same color as my pageant dress. "Now, let's get ready to go. I've got the top down in the convertible, so wear your best smile. Between you, me, and the whole town, you've got this in the bag, Savannah."

*****

At the pageant, everything happened just as I thought it would. There was the horsemanship, which Daisy and I nailed. Then, there was the fashion aspect. I wore my beautiful western outfit and paraded all around the judges. Everyone was dressed similarly, modest and looked gorgeous, but the belt buckle absolutely stole the show, with one host even asking me about it. Dixie looked so pleased in the background.

Finally, there was a short questionnaire portion while I wore my long sleeve red dress with the white cowgirl hat. It was a stunning combination, and I felt like I looked like the Wyoming version of the Statue of Liberty in full color; all that was missing was a hand torch. I had my mind clear of every distraction. I wasn't paying any mind to the people in attendance. Sure, there was a decent turnout, but since it was held during the day with the makeshift stage of the rodeo grounds sitting on top of the same dirt I barrel race on, I felt grounded. I felt comfortable. This was my element. The only thing that I was about to do that I hadn't done before was speak publicly. How hard could it really be?

"Miss Savannah." One of the judges, Terrence McCall, held up a stack of cue cards as I stepped forward. Two other women had just gone before me, but I was so busy thinking about what my questions might be and rehearsing my answers that I hadn't heard what they were asked. "How are you feeling today?" Terrence looked at me with a kindness in his eyes. He was as famous as Dixie was in Iron Spur; in fact, they used to rodeo at the same time back in the day. Rumor had it that he had been, and still was, sweet on her, too. Dixie denied all of this, having only been married once in her life and unfortunately, he died in a freak rodeo accident. She never remarried, dated, or showed any interest in romance again, according to her.

"I'm feeling—" My mind went blank as the cool breeze came to a halt. The sweltering heat hit me hard as I stood in the sudden awareness of my long sleeve dress. "Warm," was all I could croak out. Terrance broke out into a laugh, the crowd following.

"It is quite warm out here today." He fanned his face with the cue cards. "I'll keep this short for all of our sake." He smiled, shuffling through the cards while I stood still as I could because if I moved, the bead of sweat forming around the line in my hat might trickle down my face and smear my makeup.

"Thank you," I replied with my best smile. The crowd clapped in between their own fanning of themselves. This might be easier than I thought. Terrance turned away from me and faced the crowd as the American flag rose behind the stage.

"The Iron Spur Rodeo wants to take this moment to thank our troops." The crowd clapped, as a few veterans stood. I started clapping as hard as I could, looking at each soldier, young and old, to honor them. I made it through the entire crowd, when my eyes landed finally on Colter. He was here, spending his 23rd birthday watching me compete for a crown. The bead of sweat fell, and it felt like the heat got turned up even higher. I didn't know he was here, and I couldn't say that now I was better off for it. Terrance turned back to me after all of our veterans sat back down. "Savannah, Iron Spur has just gotten Colter Hays back in town." I couldn't believe this was the topic of discussion in front of the whole crowd. I hadn't even processed this fact fully for myself yet, let alone prepared anything to say publicly. I let my eyes break the gaze I shared with Terrance and stole a look at Dixie, whose expression told me everything I needed to know. She wasn't thrilled with the topic, either. Terrance continued. "What does coming home mean to you?" I released the breath I had bottled up.

"Thank you, Terrance." I started out with the canned response that Dixie had taught me to reply with before taking another deep breath. I paused, looking at the crowd, my eyes falling on Colter. "Coming home means... family." My heart skipped a beat when I wondered if that made any sense. I shook my head. Terrance kept smiling.

"I know what you mean." Terrance, clearly helping me along, spoke kindly.

"As a Christian," the crowd settled, the world grew still around me as I spoke, "I remember that we are just passing through in this world. It may be our temporary place of rest, and as much as I love Iron Spur with all of my heart and soul, we need to keep our eyes on heaven." A cool breeze finally broke through the muggy heat. The crowd took a collective sigh in response. "What I mean to say is," I paused, praying in the moment that I could make right of this jumble coming out of my mouth, "for me, home is also never losing sight of where you're going." Terrence nodded, a toothy grin across his face.

"Let's give it up for Savannah, everybody." Terrence started a clap, while his cue cards were flapping around. *Thank you, Lord for getting me through that.*

Terrence went back to the judges table, while the group deliberated. I didn't look at them while they spoke. I looked straight ahead, not allowing my eyes to wander over to Colter. Not allowing myself to give into the temptation that his face was. I was surprised he was here, certainly. My parents were in the crowd, so with glazed over eyes I scanned for them. I didn't know how I missed it before, but they were sitting in the same section as Colter. Or he was sitting in the same section as them, more likely.

Everyone in attendance was wearing red, white, and blue. It was just something people did on the Fourth of July, sure. But in Iron Spur, people took that to the next level. A day's celebration turned into weeks. The entire months of June, July, and August were for dressing patriotically. I knew I personally had more outfits that looked reminiscent of an American Flag than the average person, but the majority of residents here had me beat.

When the judges ended their deliberation, Terrence stood from the table.

"This year's Iron Spur Rodeo Queen is..." My heart sank at how quickly things were moving. "Savannah Lane." My jaw dropped.

Dixie was a fabulous coach and mentor to me. I was great in my horsemanship category. The outfits were flawless. But there were other women here who had been preparing for this for years. Their whole lives, perhaps. And here I was, just a one-off contestant, taking it all home.

Terrence came over with the crown. It had gorgeous sparkling crystals that shined brilliantly in the sunlight. A pattern of stars made up its design. Out of all the crowns I'd seen, this one had to be the most beautiful. Perhaps it was because it was mine.

As it wrapped around my hat, I felt the weight of the responsibility added along with it. Rodeo queens weren't just pageant winners; they were an embodiment of patriotism, kindness, and rodeo. I was now representing all of the things that I loved in Iron Spur. I wasn't expecting to win, nor was I expecting to feel emotions like this. My love for my country ran deeper than I ever realized before this moment.

I shook hands with the other contestants before they departed the makeshift stage. Dixie came up and handed me a bouquet of hot pink roses. My parents were cheering the loudest amongst the crowd of clapping, and I risked a glance in their direction, with Colter standing among them in cheer.

CHAPTER 15
AND THE HOME OF THE BRAVE

Colter

Pulling into the Iron Spur rodeo grounds felt surreal. I'd been in rodeo since I made the peewee division, when I could sit on a pony. Now, being back after all of these years, the emotions hit me like a brick. I put my head into my palms and prayed. *Lord, why did I have to go away?* Then, the realization came into my mind: I'd never take my home for granted again. I'd never leave Iron Spur, Wyoming again. I wanted to live here for the rest of my life, and I wanted to make it up to Savannah. Make her understand why I broke things off with her. I was afraid for my life. Getting deployed, putting my boots on foreign soil felt like the scariest thing I'd ever done. I didn't know if I was strong enough to do it. I didn't know if any second, I was going to take the wrong step and have it all be over. I didn't want Savannah to wait. I thought she'd be better off if she moved on. Forgot about me. Met someone else.

From the moment I returned home, it was clear to me that saying I wanted her to move on was in fact my worst nightmare. Though, I could never have asked her to wait for five years. That wouldn't have been fair. That wouldn't have been right. Five years was a long time to miss someone.

As I shuffled through the crowd, a lot of people were giving me pats on the back. Hands were held out to me to shake. Hugs were offered. I took them all with a graciousness and appreciation that I never knew before I became a soldier and was away from home.

As I skimmed the stands for the perfect spot to watch Savannah compete for the title of Iron Spur's rodeo queen, I made eye contact with her father. A man whom I'd often thought about. A man whom I would like to sit down with and explain myself to one day. At first, he looked away sharply, like he'd just gazed upon something he shouldn't have. But slowly, I saw his head start to move back in my direction. Finally, Savannah's mom also looked my way and immediately waved me over.

Before the contestants took the stage, we had a heart to heart. I apologized to them for the hurt I brought to Savannah.

I had been in an impossible situation. I had only wanted what was best for her. They both nodded. I asked for their forgiveness. What happened next, I never saw coming, as Savannah's mom fought back tears, and her dad hugged me.

"It's always been you, Colter," she said. "There is no one else she has loved before you or since." I felt adrenaline running through my veins as they extended their forgiveness to me. I felt empowered by the act of love they had shown me. I held back the urge to run to the dirt grounds of the arena floor and profess my undying love for her right here and now. But when the women started shuffling out, I was so taken aback by Savannah's beauty, as she was done up head to toe in clothing and style that was fit for the queen, I instead took my seat. I wanted her to have this moment. I'd taken away a lot of joy from her life with my leaving, certainly, and she deserved this opportunity to have something be about her instead.

As we watched her compete, I sat in complete awe of the beautiful woman she had grown into. She walked with grace, spoke with passion, and glowed with dignity as they went through their segments.

"Oh, happy birthday, Colter." Savannah's mom nudged me with her elbow. Her dad slapped me on the back.

"For he's a jolly good—" Savannah's mom told her husband to knock it off as he started singing. I broke out into a laugh.

"Thank you."

"Where are your folks today?" she asked me.

"Dad's firing up the barbecue, and my mom is making her ambrosia salad." I smiled at the thought. Nothing said summer like a good old-fashioned barbecue with family. "The neighbors are coming over later, then everyone will come and watch me ride tonight." I thought of how moments before, I just threw my hat back into the rodeo ring.

"Doesn't that sound swell?" Savannah's dad agreed with her mom.

"It's great that you are jumping right back in where you left off. I don't suppose you've gotten the chance to do any bull riding overseas, though." I shook my head. Being able to compete at all during the week of the Fourth was a huge deal. The fact that the rodeo board was allowing me to take my maiden voyage tonight was possibly the biggest opportunity I'd ever had, since most of the riders were in the pro rodeo circuit. The fact that I hadn't ridden since I left did worry me, but I hoped it would all come back the second I sat on the bull.

"I can skip the barbeque, if something else comes up," I said under my breath, not wanting it to sound like I didn't care about my parents, because I did. But my dad understood more than anyone how it felt to be back in civilian life right now. Like I was walking between two worlds. Like I was living a double life and trying to make sense of it all. The only thing that did make sense was the woman I was here to see.

"What time does the rodeo queen parade start?" Savannah's mom asked her dad. He looked at his watch.

"Let's see... I think it's an hour after the pageant ends, and a few hours before the rodeo starts." He nodded at her knowingly, like this was some sort of inside joke.

"That is very convenient, then. If Savannah wins, Colter could go to the parade and see the procession and still make it to his parents' barbeque. I know I can't wait to see her in Dixie's pink car, waving at the crowd." The queen always took to main street after the crowning; it was a tradition as long as the town had been here. Ever since I could remember, Dixie had been driving the winner slowly down the strip of town, behind a group of junior queens and rodeo officials on horseback. "She will be barrel racing tonight, too."

"That's a great point, dear." Savannah's dad looked at her and smiled.

"You really think so?" I asked them. "I don't want to mess things up for her and Liam." They both looked at each other and back to me.

"They broke up," her dad whispered, like the gossip might burn his tongue. "I mean, it's over for good. Not that it ever really started..." He trailed off. I knew what they meant. Liam seemed like a great guy, but what I had with Savannah was once in a lifetime. At least I hoped she still felt the same.

*****

As Savannah took the crown, I felt a pride rising up in my chest. Life had never been clearer than it was in this moment, as the Holy Spirit nudged me in her direction. I didn't know how I was going to get back with her, but I knew I had to find a way.

CHAPTER 16
AND THIS BE OUR MOTTO

Savannah

Taking the main street by storm in my brigade was magical. All of the horses were donning bright red bridles that just happened to match my dress. I smiled at Dixie in awe; surely, she had a hand in what the horses wore for the queens court. The male riders had white rose boutonnieres, and the women had white rose corsages, all of which were a nod to my white hat. For the short parade, I really did feel like royalty, as I waved to the people that we drove by.

"I'm so proud of you, Savannah," Dixie beamed, the soft hum of her classic car gliding us down the long stretch of pavement.

"I couldn't have done it without you, Dixie." She reached over and squeezed my hand that wasn't in a permanent wave. As the road came to an end, people started shuffling back inside. The town was littered with stray pieces of wrapped candy, abandoned silver shiny balloons, and assorted accessories that had fallen off of people, like hair ribbons and necklaces. The volunteer cleaning crews would come in after our drive to shovel the scattered horse droppings (a job led by the town mayor, who wore a sash while doing it—all part of the fun), kids would swarm and clean the streets of anything sugary, and any leftover confetti would remain until the wind eventually blew it away.

As we cruised, I saw customers from the diner. Family friends. My parents. And then I saw Colter's entire family, standing on the street corner in front of the ice cream shop, while Colter stood beside them. They cheered me on just as hard as everyone else, and I smiled and waved back. Having them here meant everything to me.

*****

"Now, you just have to do your inaugural barrel race tonight as our queen," Dixie said, as we pulled back up to the rodeo grounds, where my dad was there with Daisy.

"Don't I also bring out the American flag tonight, too?" I asked, and she laughed.

"Yes, I was just testing you to see if you remembered. You are the Iron Spur rodeo queen now, and you'll be riding it through the arena for all to see. And I got you the perfect outfit to wear for that occasion."

"You did? But we didn't know that I was going to win!" She reached in the back seat of her pink convertible and grabbed a paper bag, pulling out a sequined fringe jacket.

"Oh, I knew you would win, Savannah. You are the perfect representation of Iron Spur." My heart leapt at the beautiful jacket. I was also pleased how thin the material was—like a dancer's costume, so it could be worn in the heat, but it still looked luxurious.

"I can't thank you enough for all of this." I leaned across the bucket seat and gave her a hug.

"You're welcome, dear. Now go; I know you have more going on today than just this." She winked, and I shimmied in my long dress and boots to get out of the car. I couldn't wait to change my clothes. I needed a cold shower to cool off. I needed a huge drink of water. I needed to see Colter—having him at my events today felt both exciting and nerve wracking. It was hard to put my feelings into words. Just because he was all I ever wanted, didn't mean he didn't feel like a stranger to me now. And

I still felt bad about Liam. Though he was just a brief moment in time in my life, I didn't ever want to hurt him, and I prayed that I could learn from that mistake.

*****

That night, at the biggest rodeo of the year—on our nation's 250th birthday, no less—I donned my best jeans, a white short-sleeve top that was tucked in, and the red, white, and blue fringe sequined jacket. Dixie also let me wear the large silver buckle again for the overall look. My white hat glistened with its crown, and I'd never felt more beautiful. Despite my mixed emotions about Colter, having him back here was the icing on the cake. This was shaping up to be the best Fourth of July I'd ever experienced as I rode through the arena with the crowd cheering, holding up the American flag as high as I could.

The first event of the evening was calf roping, starting with the junior league. It went off without a hitch, ending with a winner who broke the previous year's record held by Iron Spur resident Jimmy Mills.

Next up was barrel racing. I swapped out my hat for one without the crown, handing it off to Dixie who was with me behind the scenes tonight to "protect the rhinestones," as she teased. Really, she wanted to keep my crown in a box for safekeeping while I competed, and for that, I couldn't be more thankful. I still donned the same outfit, only pulling my hair back so it didn't get caught on anything while Daisy and I raced as fast as we could around the barrels. It wasn't my best time overall, but at the end of the event, I won second place. A spot I was more than thrilled to get.

Bronc riding happened for twenty minutes or so while I went back to the contestant stands, crown back on my head. Dixie sat with me while she recited from memory every contestant's previous score that they've ever gotten. There was no one here who took rodeo more seriously than Dixie.

The last event of the night was bull riding. I looked over at my parents, as this was my dad's ultimate event to watch. He could never do the bull riding himself due to an old football injury back in the day, but he resonated with the sport more than anything. Seeing him now, I was surprised to see that his eyes weren't locked on the overhead display naming off the contestants, but instead, he was looking at me. Then I heard the announcer say it.

"Up next, we have our own Colter Hays! He's just returned from five years in the Army and is eager to reclaim his stakes in the sport that he showed much promise in, all those years ago." My heart dropped. I didn't know about this. Of course, I was thrilled about him getting back into rodeo. Heck, that was where we met. But I was also nervous. Bull riding was a dangerous game, and I just hoped he was really ready for this after all the time away.

I felt my body standing—I can't help it—I had to see him in the shoots. There he was, wearing the helmet and body armor, sitting on the bull that was enclosed by the gate. Any second now, the shoot would open and, before I could imagine what would be, it did. The crowd went wild during bull riding more than it did for any sport. I was right there with them—praying, cheering, screaming at the top of my lungs for Colter to hold on. To hold on with everything he had.

Seconds felt like hours as the bull kicked and jumped, using all of its strength to try and remove the rider from its back, but Colter defied all odds. Not all of the bulls were the same—some were less ornery than others, but this bull was definitely on the extreme end of angst. He wasn't happy about any of this, but still, Colter gripped that animal with a strength in his legs that I'd call heroic, with one arm in the air per the regulations of the sport.

"Six," the announcer screamed out into the arena. "Seven! EIGHT!" Colter did it. Eight seconds passed, and now it was time for him to safely eject himself. I watched him dismount. He fumbled a little, falling backwards, and my heart stopped in suspense. The crowd silenced in pause, as the bull was close. Too close. The bull could have easily stomped his leg or ran over him, but thankfully, the rodeo clowns were on it and quickly gave the bull something else to chase, as they came running over to the animal before jumping into barrels. Colter stood on his feet as the crowd went wild.

"And just like that—it's like Colter Hays never left Iron Spur!" The announcer screamed over the arena, the freshly kicked up dirt in the air bringing back all of the emotions from when he did leave. I had the scars on my heart to prove he had been gone, but now, along with the rest of Iron Spur, his leaving did feel like some sort of dream that I finally woke up from.

CHAPTER 17
IN GOD IS OUR TRUST

Savannah

After the Rodeo

My dad met me in the back parking lot and helped load up Daisy. Since my parents could see the drone firework show from their ranch, and they didn't want me out driving tonight with all of the town partying, they took Daisy back with them, so I didn't have to. I kissed her on her nose before they left, hugging my dad to thank him. My mom came out from the grandstands after chatting with a few of their friends. They both congratulated me on the perfect evening, and we said our goodbyes.

I could see my apartment from here, as I stood alone for the first time today. I had been swarmed with people since I woke up—actually, all week. This was the first moment I'd had since Colter got back that I truly had nowhere to be, no one to see, or no one whom I needed to greet. Shake hands with. Shmooze. Now what? The fireworks didn't start for a few minutes, still. I could go back to my apartment and change my clothes, but I felt good in this outfit. I could go to the contestant's tent and get a Gatorade or water, but I'd have to walk through the crowd of people to get there. Then, I realized I could avert the crowd by walking around the back of the grandstands and get a drink that way. I followed suit, disappearing from the parking lot and walking the road alone.

I wasn't ten steps into my journey when I saw Colter, clearly thinking the same as I did about not wanting to talk to a lot of people. Seeing him made every vein in my body feel like a super-highway for electricity. Watching him tonight made me feel alive in ways that I couldn't explain. The magic of the Fourth of July in Iron Spur made things sparkle in new ways, and tonight, I was feeling that with an intensity I'd never felt before. Colter stopped when he saw me walking.

"Happy birthday," I said. He paused like he wasn't expecting that.

"Thanks." His voice was so quiet, I almost missed it. The energy between us was intense. Just being near him made me feel weak in the knees. "Will you spend it with me?" My heart felt like it was playing tennis at Wimbledon. I looked around, as if I had any reason to say no. As if I wanted to say no. I only wanted to say yes to this man for the rest of my life, even though we had years between us to catch up on.

"Yes, I will," I said without hesitation. Without anything holding me back. He smiled bigger than I'd ever seen, and somehow, we were back to where we were all those years ago. I felt like I was sixteen again.

"Do you trust me?" he asked. A question I'd heard before. A smile crossed my face before I nodded. "Good."

We went to the drink tent and grabbed a few bottles of water and some Gatorade, rehydrating from the heat and the rodeo that we both just competed in. After we both drank as much as we could, he ushered me out of the tent.

"I have an idea," he whispered, taking my hand in his. The electricity of his touch made me feel like I might collapse, but I used all my strength to stay upright. This had been a very long day, and my legs felt weak after my barrel race, but he picked up his pace, and I followed. We ran back to where all of the horses were, in the dirt area of the parking lot, and it was just like it was all those years ago.

The man was standing there as if he was waiting for us. Two horses, dressed in a sparkling regalia, were saddled and ready to ride. The man was smiling ear to ear as he looked upon us, now a rodeo queen and a soldier. An up-and-coming champion bull rider if he wanted to be.

"How did you pull this off again?" I asked Colter, who just smiled as he made the same arrangements with the man as last time, and we both got into the saddles of the beautiful horses with coats that shined with a luster like they were dipped in gold.

We rode the quiet streets as the drone fireworks began in the background—a show tonight that would go on for hours for America's 250th. A show tonight that would probably last until early tomorrow morning if I knew Iron Spur. But as we sauntered through the empty streets littered with glittering confetti, my emotions started to change.

"Are you just going to pretend you never left?" I asked. It was a loaded question, and part of me didn't want to ruin the evening. The other part of me was ready to get to the meat of this. Colter looked ahead. The expression on his face was unreadable. He looked both happy and sad—the reflection of how I felt.

"I'm sorry, Savannah."

"It's not that you left—I respect that you did. It's that you changed your tune so quickly and ended things with me." I brought my horse to a slow, wanting to talk this over with him face to face. The street benches we sat on with our hot dogs before were right next to us. I dismounted from the saddle and led my horse over to the light post, letting it stand and graze on the park grass. Colter hesitated but followed suit.

Emotion hit me like a brick. Suddenly, I was both angry and sad. Happy but crying. A whirlwind of feelings as tears ran down my cheeks.

"I would have waited for you!" I shouted now, not able to contain it. "I did wait for you." Colter tried to put his arms around me, but I pushed him away.

"I didn't want you to wait for me... In case I didn't get to come home." His words hit like an anvil falling from the sky. Suddenly... I understood the man standing before me. He was still the boy I fell in love with, but now he'd seen things and put his life on the line in situations that most wouldn't. He did it for the country he loved. He did it for the people who were blessed to call this country home. He did it for me. "I didn't want your life tied to that kind of ending." I turned around, facing him, and he was just inches from me. I leaned into him, clinging to his body with the intensity that I only dreamt about in all these years without him. My hat toppled off my head, bouncing in the grass. I didn't care. I didn't care about any of it. He let go of our tight embrace to retrieve it for me. Letting go of his body felt like taking off a winter coat—it didn't matter how warm it was, but my body had gotten used to the temperature of the jacket, and I wanted it back.

"Savannah," Colter said, placing the hat with my crown back on my head and running his fingers through my long strawberry hair. "If you forgive me, I promise I will spend the rest of my life making it up to you. I'm not going anywhere ever again. I want to be here, in Iron Spur, with you. Forever." I didn't need to think about it. I didn't need any more words. I just needed him. We both embraced one another again, but this time, his lips met mine as the fireworks glittered in the distance.

ABOUT THE AUTHOR

Cassandra discovered her passion for writing at the age of seven when she purchased a diary at the Scholastic Book Fair. What began with journal entries about her school and home life later evolved into a collection of poems, short stories, and novels. Her hobbies include skiing, traveling around the Rocky Mountains, and reading. Much of her writing inspiration stems from her love of dogs, her Onondaga heritage, and her Christian faith. Cassandra's favorite genres of books are Christian fiction novels, Thrillers, and anything British. She is a full-time writer and resides in the mountains of Wyoming with her husband, Chad.

OTHER BOOKS

Giddy Up, Gorgeous: A Clean, No-Spice Christian Romcom
Lights, Camera... Yeehaw.

Hollywood starlet Sadie Clark has it all—beauty, talent, and a phone that never stops ringing. That is, until her cowboy-actor boyfriend dumps her in a viral social media post, and her red-hot career goes ice-cold overnight. Now, the only job she's offered is a low-budget film on a Wyoming dude ranch. It's not what she planned—but she's surprised by how much she loves it... and by the real cowboy who's impossible to ignore. Somewhere between heartache and "yeehaw," she discovers her worth doesn't come from headlines, and that God's script is always better than her own.

A Ranger, A Wolf, and a Really Bad Tent: A Clean, No-Spice Christian Romcom

When her phone dies in Yellowstone, she just might find a real connection.

Ember Hollis is addicted to her phone and chasing relevance when a sudden microburst floods her Yellowstone campsite and waterlogs the one thing she can't live without. Forced offline, she collides with Ridge Sawyer: a rugged, very hot park ranger with cowboy roots, muscles for days, and no cell phone at all.

As the wilderness strips away the filters, Ember is forced to face herself. And while the park buzzes over a legendary wolf returning to Yellowstone for her mate, Ember discovers a deeper love—one that leads her not just to a man, but back to Christ.

Howdy, Handsome: An All-Space, No-Spice Christian Romcom

Houston, We Have A... Meet-Cute.

When a test flight goes sideways, astronaut Jack Carter crash-lands in the last place he expected: the middle of a Wyoming cattle ranch. Dazed, suffering from amnesia, and drop-dead handsome- he can't remember his mission- or even his own name.

Enter Annie McGraw, a cowgirl who doesn't have time for stray cattle... Let alone stray astronauts. But when she takes him in, sparks fly faster than a rocket launch. Out under Wyoming's star-filled skies, Jack launches into a mission he never trained for: a woman who just might be his greatest adventure yet, and a faith that grounds him more than gravity ever could.

The Chalet Next Door: An All-Ski, No-Spice Christian Romcom

Blizzard Outside. Banter Inside. Sparks Inevitable.

Bubbly book publisher Presley Astor has been told all her life she's "too much." But she's perfectly happy being herself- and taking her pampered Shih Tzu, Priscilla, on a solo ski trip to Sage Mountain, Wyoming. What she's not prepared for is a blizzard knocking out her power and forcing her to seek refuge in the chalet next door...with a brooding cowboy who clearly doesn't know what to do with someone like her. Ford Prescott is a guarded skijoring champion-a rodeo sport where a horse pulls a skier at breakneck speeds-preparing for the biggest race of his life. But he's also fighting cheating competitors and a faith that's quietly slipping through his fingers. As snow piles high and the town shuts down, Presley's joy (and Priscilla's undeniable charm) begins melting Ford's walls. But when old insecurities and misunderstandings hit harder than the storm, they'll have to decide if God's plan for them is bigger than just surviving the blizzard.

How to Fall for a Cowboy: An All-Pumpkin, No-Spice Christian Romcom

She's Glossy Nails. He's Flakey Crust. The Plan? Half-Baked.

In the town of Maple Haven, Wyoming, Autumn isn't just a season- it's a celebration. Ginger Hart is spending the season like she has for the past year: hopelessly crushing on Dallas, the gym bro who communicates in motivational quotes. In her quest for his attention, Ginger's lost more than a few pounds- maybe, a bit of herself. As the town gears up for the annual Pumpkin Stampede, something (or rather someone) rolls into town in a pumpkin-themed dessert truck parked right outside Ginger's salon. Behind the counter? Ex bull-rider Tucker Callahan. He's all cowboy hat and delicious sweets- basically everything Ginger's been trying to resist. When they decide to fake date for his image and for her to get Dallas' attention, he proposes one sugary-sweet condition. As cozy sparks fly, Ginger begins to wonder if God's sweetest plans aren't always the ones we bake up ourselves.

A Weather Girl's Guide to Love: A Thunderously Sweet Christian Romcom

Partly Cloudy, Mostly Complicated.

Hailey Sinclair had her life all mapped out- until God changed the forecast. Instead of being an on-air meteorologist for a national network, she's reporting the weather in rural Wyoming. Now she's caught between her college sweetheart, Jett Dawson, and Colt Wilder- the infuriatingly gorgeous and cheerful cameraman who seems determined to break through her stormy exterior. Torn between the future she planned, and the one God might be writing, Hailey must learn to trust His direction- and her heart- even when it leads straight into the eye of the storm.

A New Leash on Life: A Dog-Mom Rom-Com, Book 1

Get ready for a hilarious Christian romantic comedy as we follow the journey of a thirty-something introverted woman, Katie Fitzgerald, who's longing for a husband. But when she accidentally adopts a dog, she discovers that love comes in unexpected ways, and that God's timing is always perfect.

Fetching Love: A Dog-Mom Rom-Com, Book 2

Three couples, three journeys, and one hilarious adventure on the unpredictable path to love. Katie and Eli are ready to say "I do," but the days leading up to the wedding are full of surprises- especially when Katie's mom's true crime sleuthing lands her in a pickle. Samantha and Mitchell seem perfect together, but hidden struggles test their relationship. Can they find common ground, or will their opposing desires pull them apart? Carolyn and Micah have found faith and each other, but their surprise romance leads to a sudden, life- altering decision. As these couples follow the Lord, they find joy and laughter along the way.

The Après-Ski Proposal: A Romcom About Love Off-Piste

She came for a fresh start... Not a fake boyfriend. When Claire Riley gets dumped on the eve of her 30th birthday, she's blindsided. A spur-of-the-moment ski trip seems like the perfect escape, until she runs into her ex... With his new girlfriend.

Shocked and desperate for a lifeline, Claire accepts a proposal from a charming stranger to pose as her fake- boyfriend. What begins as a simple act of saving face turns into a journey that reveals a fresh start in life and love—the kind that only God could have planned.

www.ingramcontent.com/pod-product-compliance
Lightning Source LLC
Chambersburg PA
CBHW062213150726
47991CB00006B/2267